Roya.

CW00386128

Lion

Zoe Chant

Also by Zoe Chant

Fire & Rescue Shifters

Firefighter Dragon

Firefighter Pegasus

Firefighter Griffin

1

SIGNY

Signy Zlotsky was not going to cry on the bus.

She shoved the stupid plastic nametag from her first day working at a grocery store pharmacy into her pocket. She wasn't going to stare at the CINDY printed there, or renamed Signy, saying, "What good's a nametag no one can read?"

Signy hadn't argued. She already knew that it didn't help when she said her name was pronounced exactly the way it looked: *Sig-nee*. Her name looked strange, and strangers rarely even bothered to try pronouncing it. People who did—who said *Sign-ee* or *Sing-y* or her personal favorite, a vaguely French *Sin-yee*—at least saw her and her weird foreign name and took a shot. Her own family mostly called her *Siggy*, which she felt weird offering to others as a nickname; it sounded either babyish or a little too David Bowie for a grown woman who was far too curvaceous to pull off a Ziggy Stardust look.

Strangers mostly didn't want to be bothered, though, so they said *Sandy* or *Cindy*. And Signy let them, especially when it was her first day at a new job, and the person casually renaming her was her boss.

She wasn't going to think about that, though. She wasn't going to cry on the bus, and she wasn't going to think about how easily she could be fired and replaced with some other pharmacy tech with barely any experience.

I just want someone to care enough to say my name right, Signy thought, leaning her forehead against the glass. *I just want someone to care whether I'm there at all.*

The bus stopped and people got on; Signy looked up automatically to scan the people boarding. She stood up from her seat to make room for a harried looking woman with two young children.

The woman didn't seem to even see her, just herding the children toward the suddenly empty seat. Signy planted her feet in the aisle and pulled her phone out of her pocket, checking again for any messages or emails.

The last text in her conversation with her little sister, Poppy, was still her own, from two days ago. *Happy birthday, Pops!*

It was no surprise that Poppy, who took after their mother in her slim build and brilliant red hair as well as her constant searching for something new somewhere else, hadn't replied. Signy knew Poppy was fine She had posted a picture on Instagram that Signy had seen on her lunch break, showing a glorious multicolored sunset over a vast ocean.

Signy, sitting in a fluorescent-lit break room, alone except for a grim gray-haired cashier intently watching *Judge Judy*, had had to Google where in the world the sun was setting at that hour. She had concluded that it was probably the Indian Ocean, or maybe the Mediterranean. Poppy's "year off" from college was looking like a lifestyle at this point—a constant whirl of new places, new faces, new adventures. Poppy's adventures were like all the travels of their childhood on constant fast forward.

All Signy wanted was to have a home she could call her own, and someone there with her at the end of the day. Someone who could make her forget that no one else in the world seemed to know her name. Someone who would make a home with her in one place, not feeling bored or tied down but safe and secure.

Someone who might even make dinner when she worked the late shift, and maybe after dinner...

Signy shook her head, smiling to herself. Fantasizing about some imaginary boyfriend on the bus was better than crying on the bus, but not by much. She imagined telling her mom, or Poppy, what she wanted.

She knew what either of them would say: *It's too long since you went on a date! Go out! Live a little!*

Signy glanced around the bus, wondering if one of the men around her would turn out to be perfect for her if she just struck up a conversation. Somehow she doubted it. She hadn't been with anyone in over a year, and she didn't want yet another awkward first date. She could hardly imagine a one night stand, hooking up at a bar or a party the way other people seemed to think was perfectly normal. She just wanted someone to go home to, someone who would stay with her.

Too bad you can't skip all the getting-to-know-you and go straight to happily married, Signy thought, looking up just in time to see that her stop was next. She pocketed her phone again and maneuvered toward the door. *I wish I could just pick someone. I wonder if matchmakers are still a thing, somewhere?*

But that still might not work, of course—Signy had tried with a couple of boyfriends in the past. She had told herself she was sure and this was it, but it never was.

She stepped off the bus into the muggy heat of a September that thought it was still August, and thought again about moving somewhere cooler. She'd settled herself in Wisconsin partly because she was born here, and

3

partly because she thought it had to be cooler there, but the humid Midwestern summer in a barely air-conditioned upstairs flat had cured her of that idea.

She turned the corner onto her block, a long row of cookie cutter houses and duplexes built in the fifties, a corner of the city with all the personality of the suburbs. Her downstairs neighbors were nice enough, but they were busy with their jobs and with each other, plus a baby due in the winter. She had barely met anyone else on the street, just waving and smiling when someone happened to be outside as she was walking to or from the bus stop.

Signy stopped short when she realized that there was a sleek black car parked in front of her duplex. Did her neighbors have company? She didn't know if she could bear to hear them laughing and chatting with friends. It would only make Signy more aware of how far she was from a life like that—married and looking forward to a baby, with everything all worked out.

She was still standing there, debating turning around and getting back on the bus, or at least going to a coffee shop for a few hours, when a man in a suit stepped out of the car. He stood there on the grass at the edge of the street and looked right at her.

He had gray hair and gray eyes in a pale, weathered face, wearing a suit that looked somehow both expensive and not-from-around-here. He had a little gold pin in his tie, and two rings on his right hand, none on his left.

"Signy Zlotsky?"

Signy's jaw dropped a little at the thought that he was here for *her* as much as the fact that he said her name—both of them!—perfectly correctly.

He took a half step forward while she was still standing there trying to gather her wits. He repeated impatiently, "You are Signy Zlotsky?"

He had a slight accent, she realized, and it sounded faintly, strangely familiar. But she'd also had *quite enough* of people getting impatient with her before she'd had half a

4

second to think. She wasn't getting paid to take anybody's bad attitude with a smile now.

Signy folded her arms over her work-issued green polo shirt and set her feet firmly on the sidewalk. "Who's asking?"

"My name is Otto Sparre af Varg," he said haughtily. "I am an advisor to your grandfather—your *true* father's father. He has sent me to speak with you."

Signy felt her face set into a scowl, squaring her shoulders, even though she also felt terribly curious.

Her father, her mother's first husband and the guy responsible for saddling her with a first name no one in America could pronounce on sight, had died when she was just two years old. Her mom had married Frank Zlotsky before Signy turned four, and Poppy had been born a year later. She didn't remember any dad but Frank, and she didn't like people telling her who her *true* father was.

But no one had ever told her she had a grandfather.

"I will ask again." Otto took another step forward. "You are Signy Zlotsky, are you not? Born Signy Bjornsson, the daughter of Nikolas and Mary Bjornsson?"

His accent sounded like her father's, she was suddenly certain. But that didn't make any sense. She didn't remember her father at all. She'd made up stories about him when she was little, but she had been too young to really remember anything. The stories had been just childish fantasies.

Hadn't they?

"Yes," Signy said, unfolding her arms, glancing toward the gleaming car. "Yes, I'm Signy Zlotsky. That's my name."

"Your name, as your father gave it to you," Otto said, "is Signy Marija Victoria Aspenas af Bjorn. And as I said, I come with an important message from your grandfather; shall we shout his private business in the street, or will you invite me in?"

Otto flicked a hand at the duplex, and Signy glanced

toward it. If you weren't familiar with the way houses were divided into flats, it wouldn't be obvious that there were two apartments in it.

She tried to imagine taking Otto up the stairs to her second-story apartment. It would be nice to watch him sweat in that suit, but Signy knew she would feel like a bad hostess to her uninvited guest rather than enjoying his discomfort.

And there was something about him, all lean and silver, watching her with that impatient expression. He was being polite, barely, but he obviously expected her to just do whatever he wanted her to because he said so.

Signy shook her head. "I don't invite strange men into my home, even if they claim to know some grandfather I've never heard of who hasn't sent me a birthday card in twenty-five years."

Otto huffed but turned toward the car. "In here, then. Allow *me* to extend an invitation, and I shall present my credentials."

Signy took a few cautious steps after him. It wasn't a good idea to get in strangers' cars, either, no matter what cheerful stories Poppy told her about her adventures in hitchhiking. On the other hand, who would go to this much trouble to get Signy alone? Otto's story was weird, but it made more sense than any other reason for this to be happening.

The car was parked facing away, and all the rear windows were tinted; Signy was nearly level with the door before she spotted the suited shoulder of a man sitting in the front seat and stopped again. Otto had already opened the back door, and was gesturing her in; she could feel the seductive coolness of the air conditioning running on full blast. The seats were black leather, and there was a briefcase on the nearest seat.

Signy bent over to peer through the front window, getting a glimpse of the two big men, much younger than Otto, sitting in the driver and passenger seats up front.

Both of them were wearing suits and sunglasses. The driver had tan skin and tawny blond hair, and the man riding shotgun had brown skin and black curly hair. Both of them stared straight ahead.

Signy backed up a step. "If I'm going to sit in a car with a stranger, I'm taking the driver's seat. I'm not letting your armed guards just drive off with me whenever you decide."

Otto made an irritated noise, but he reached into the car and knocked on a little divider, like in a cab, between the back and front seats. Both men opened their doors, and Signy backed up a couple more steps as they got out, trying to watch both of them at once and wondering if anyone would come outside if she screamed.

"Keep watch out here," Otto said to them, reaching into the car and grabbing the briefcase. "The lady has requested privacy."

Both men nodded, and Signy caught the gleam of sunlight on sweat trickling down the blond one's neck. She felt bad for a moment, banishing them to stand outside in the heat in their black suits—but she wasn't about to get herself kidnapped just because it was gorgeous and slightly sweaty men in suits looking to do it. The guards moved back to the sidewalk, and Signy slid into the driver's seat.

It was still warm from the big blond man's body heat, a startling contrast to the chilly air of the car. It felt strangely intimate, as though she were sitting in his lap, and Signy glanced out through the windshield after him. He had turned away, and was walking up the driveway while the black-haired man stood perfectly still on the sidewalk.

Otto slid into the passenger seat beside her. Signy shut her door, focusing again on him.

He popped open the briefcase in his lap and fished out a letter and a passport. "As I said, my credentials."

The letter was on heavy paper with some kind of logo on top in full color—a gold crown above a red shield with two yellow trees, with white bears to either side of the shield holding it up.

Aspenas for aspen trees, she heard someone saying, a familiar voice with a familiar slight accent. *And 'af Bjorn' means of the bear, our clan. Where we come from, polar bears are just the normal kind of bear.*

Signy touched the crest, feeling strangely close to crying, as her eyes skimmed down past some writing in an alphabet she couldn't read to the start of the letter.

To our beloved if rarely-seen granddaughter, Signy, Greetings, We have sent Count Otto Sparre af Varg as our emissary

"Count?" Signy asked, her gaze flicking up to the crown over the crest again, and down to the end of the letter. The printed words gave the name of the writer, just one despite all the "we" and "our."

Einar Magnus Henrik, King of Valtyra

Signy looked over at him again, her eyes widening.

"That is my title," Otto—Count Otto? What was she supposed to call him?—agreed. "And I sit on the King's Council as his First Minister."

"The King," Signy repeated, looking down at the letter again. Her grandfather, a king. Her father, a prince.

Signy remembered suddenly, the first time she held Poppy. She had looked up at her mother and asked if Poppy was a princess too.

"Poppy's an American citizen, just like you and me," her mother had said. "We're proud to be Americans. We don't need any princes and princesses here, we have a democracy."

But Signy was suddenly sure that there was a reason she'd asked that question. She thought she could remember her father's voice, calling her *princess* and meaning something different from all the millions of other fathers who called their daughters the same thing.

"I don't understand," Signy said, even though she

thought she did understand. She thought that if someone gave her a map she could put her finger on the place Valtyra was, in the middle of the North Sea, even though it never showed up on maps unless she colored it in.

"Your grandfather is king of Valtyra, and both his sons have now died," Otto said briskly. "His only remaining heir is you, Signy Marija Victoria Aspenas af Bjorn."

He handed another heavy sheet of paper across to her. The top line was the strange alphabet she couldn't read—runes?—but the next line read REGISTRATION OF BIRTH. It listed her own birthday, and the long version of her name Otto had kept repeating. Not typed, like her familiar ordinary birth certificate, but written in a hand she had seen a few times before, on the backs of photos and the inside covers of a few old books.

It was her father's writing.

He had indicated where Signy was born, and that was the same as her birth certificate: Froedtert Hospital, Milwaukee, Wisconsin.

The next line gave her mother's full name as *Mary Margaret Arnott Bjornsson*, and to her surprise she saw her mother's signature there. That meant her mother had seen this other birth certificate. Whatever this proved, her mother already knew.

The next line gave her father's full name in a form Signy had never seen before: *Alexander Gustav Frederik Aspenäs af Bjorn, called Bjornsson, Prince of Valtyra.*

Signy's hands began to shake, making it hard to read the rest of the page, a few lines of writing like nothing on her birth certificate. The first few lines were in runes, but the next were in English—probably a translation.

I accept from my son this report of the birth of his daughter and heir, and bestow upon her the title Princess Signy of Valtyra, Countess of Nordholm.
Einar Magnus Henrik, King of Valtyra

9

Princess, just like her father had called her when she was very small. Just like her mother had told her she wasn't anymore.

This was impossible. It couldn't be true. And at the same time it answered questions Signy had never really thought to ask, about why she seemed to have no family at all beyond her mother, stepfather, and baby sister.

Signy looked down at the paper again. It should have seemed like no proof at all—anyone could make up something like this, couldn't they? But she touched her mother's signature, familiar from a lifetime of permission slips and checks, and her own real—American—birth certificate. She could feel where the pen had indented the paper.

"Why was I never told?" Signy asked. "Why..."

"Your father followed your mother away from his kingdom, because *she* did not wish to live the life of a princess in Valtyra. He died like—"

"Don't you dare," Signy blurted. One of the few things she did have of her father were the newspaper clippings about his death; he had been struck by a car while trying to help a woman stranded on the side of the road. Otto might think that wasn't a sufficiently heroic death for a Prince of Valtyra, but Signy wouldn't let anyone speak badly of her father.

Otto waved it away like it didn't matter. "Your mother didn't wish to bring you to Valtyra either. Your grandfather allowed it because he had another heir, but your uncle died a few weeks ago, childless, and we had no alternative but to seek you out. You are an adult, you can make your own choice now. You are a wealthy woman, Your Highness, regardless of what you may ultimately inherit from the King. You are Countess of Nordholm in your own right; you have holdings attached to that title."

Signy shook her head. "I don't understand. You... what, you want me to come to Valtyra and... and be the next queen? Rule some country I've never heard of?"

10

Otto snorted. "No, Your Highness, of course no one expects you to actually rule. Even if you had lived in Valtyra all your life, you lack certain... qualifications."

Signy twisted toward him, angry again after all those shocks in a row. "What, you mean... because I'm female?"

Otto shook his head. "No, Your Highness. Because like your mother, and unlike your father and his father before him, you are entirely human."

It should have sounded crazier than every other thing he'd said. She should have laughed it off, no matter how nice his suit and his briefcase and his car, no matter how coolly he said it.

But just like his accent, just like her grandfather's crest, there was something she recognized in Otto's words. She looked down at the page in her hands again, the registration of birth. Her father's name, and hers. Not *Bjornsson*, but *af Bjorn*. The polar bears who held up the shield in the crest.

Our clan. The bear.

She thought of one of the few pictures she'd seen of herself with her father. He had been a big man, tall and broad, with dark hair and eyes that contrasted sharply with his fair skin and rosy cheeks. She remembered the deep rumble of his voice. She remembered him asking her a question.

"Can you do it, bjornunge? Show Papa. Can you?"

She had tried. She had tried and tried to show him what he wanted to see, but nothing ever happened. And then she had said, "You do it, Papa."

Her Papa had laughed his low rumbling laugh and said, "All right, princess, all right, I'll show you one more time."

And then her father got down on his hands and knees and rubbed his nose against hers. She squeezed her eyes shut and when she opened them, her father had been replaced by an enormous white bear, still with her father's familiar dark eyes, just like hers.

Signy opened her eyes, but Otto was still watching her with his very human expression of impatience. *Wolf,* she

11

thought. *Varg is the wolf, as Bjorn is the bear.*

She looked out the window toward the guards. The blond one was still out of sight, but she remembered his size and the obvious power of him. The black-haired guard also radiated strength where he stood on the sidewalk. What were they? What shapes would they take?

"My father..." Signy said, and it struck her in a way that it hadn't for a long time that he was dead.

Her father, the bear prince living quietly in America with his human wife and human daughter, her father who called her *bjornunge*—bear cub—and *princess*, was dead. She had thought she forgot him, thought she never really knew him enough to miss him, but grief washed over her suddenly. Her throat went tight and tears sprang to her eyes, but she knew that crying in front of Otto would be a thousand times worse than crying on the bus.

She shoved the driver's side door open and bolted out into the street, running down the block as fast as she could. She ignored Otto's shouts behind her. She couldn't let her tears fall until she was somewhere safe, and that meant getting far away from the wolf.

2

KAI

Kai was sweating as soon as he and Tristan were evicted from the car by Otto's peremptory demand. He barely let his eyes touch upon Princess Signy, who was managing to look regal, or at least unimpressed with Otto, in khaki pants and a short-sleeved green shirt that clung to her generous curves.

Kai didn't let himself look closer than that. He turned away, scanning the area around them for eavesdroppers or threats to the princess.

Threats to Otto, Kai wouldn't mind so much. As a member of the Royal Guard, he was only sworn to protect the royal family. Otto could look out for himself.

Then Otto shut himself in the car with the princess. Kai was alone on the street with his fellow guard, Tristan, whose black curls were looking particularly wild in this humid air. Tristan was apparently too dignified to look troubled by the heat; the corner of his mouth twitched up faintly, which for Tristan was the equivalent of a belly laugh at Kai's discomfort.

"I'm going to check in with Magnus, report that we've made contact with Her Highness," Kai said, with what dignity he could muster.

Tristan gave a tiny fraction of a nod as Kai strode away up the driveway, checking that the backyard of the princess's home was as empty and quiet as the front. There was a shaded spot near the back of the house where he had a partial view of the street. He could see the front of the rental car, and would see anyone approaching up the street from the west.

He slipped on an earpiece and reached into his pocket to dial home with a few taps of his fingers. He and Tristan were the only guards dispatched on this mission with Otto; the Royal Guard had shrunk in the last several years. The Royal Family had consisted for so long of only the king and the crown prince that they didn't need many guards, and anyway there were few who were willing to take the oaths and renounce their own names and titles in the king's service.

Magnus, the Captain of the Guard, had been trying for years to get permission to assign a guard to Princess Signy, or to find her and contact her. The Crown Prince had blocked them, still jealous of his younger brother twenty years after his death. The king had acceded to his son's wishes, and the Royal Guard had had no choice but to obey the king.

Magnus picked up on the first ring. The sound of someone speaking Valtyran was almost as welcome as a cool breeze off the sea would have been. "Kai! How is America? Are you enjoying your first trip abroad?"

It had come out, when Magnus was choosing who to assign, that Kai had never left Valtyra before, beyond a few brief family trips when he was too young to shift. Most Valtyrans spent some time abroad—especially if they were shifters and hadn't yet met their mate. Kai, insisting on studying in Valtyra rather than going off to college, had once said, *If my mate is going to take me away from Valtyra, I don't want to find her.*

Many shifters left Valtyra nowadays to hide among humans all over the world, but Kai loved his island home. Shifter traditions might seem strange and archaic to outsiders, but Valtyra was a place where shifters had no need to hide their natures, where all shifters lived peacefully under the rule of their king. Kai loved Valtyra, and he would do anything to protect it.

He would even leave it, for a little while, when ordered to do so. Magnus had needed someone with an understanding of royal and noble politics to keep an eye on Otto and Princess Signy. This was certainly no time to wonder if his mate might be wandering around this foreign place, waiting to be found. Kai had to focus on protecting the princess and the king, and through them all of Valtyra.

"It's hot," Kai returned shortly. "But we've found Her Highness. Otto is explaining things to her now."

"Do you think she'll agree to come home quickly?"

Kai thought of the way Princess Signy had stood on the sidewalk, staring Otto down. It was early evening; if she had been coming home from her job she had been working late. But she had still stood strong when facing a wolf in a finely-cut suit.

"She did not seem... overly trusting," Kai said cautiously, knowing he had to be careful of what he said, just as Magnus did. The Royal Guard was charged with the protection of the royal family, and strictly forbidden from meddling in politics.

Kai hadn't ever heard anyone say that it might be their duty to protect the king from his own First Minister. Things were not as clear-cut as that yet. But Kai knew that Magnus was hoping this mission would keep Otto in America for some time. Even a full day and night would provide an opening for others to try to speak to him about the influence Otto wielded.

"Well, let her know when you have the chance that you

have come for *her* protection, not Otto's—"

There was a sharp sound, and Kai hung up the call as he darted forward. He was in time to see Princess Signy burst out of the black car and run down the street, papers fluttering away as she went.

"*Those are Royal documents!*" Otto snarled.

Tristan glanced toward Kai as he moved toward the street in the direction of Otto's furiously pointing finger.

Kai nodded and ran in the opposite direction, chasing Princess Signy. If they'd come all this way to find her, only to scare her into running out in front of a car...

Kai's lion roared, eager to stretch his legs and give chase, and Kai forgot all about the heat as he ran, though the woman he chased was the furthest thing from prey. She didn't look back, seeming not to notice that she was pursued, but she looked left and right when she reached a cross street. Kai was close enough behind to be sure that there was no traffic to be worried about.

She ran straight across and onto the sidewalk, turning right when she got there without slackening her pace. Kai followed her for a few paces, then drew even before she could notice him behind her and be frightened.

"Ma'am," he said, keeping his gaze straight ahead as though he were in full uniform on some ceremonial duty when Princess Signy's head whipped around toward him. He concentrated on speaking English to her rather than Valtyran. "My name is Kai, and I'm a lieutenant in the Royal Guard of Valtyra, sent for your protection. Can you tell me where we're going?"

Princess Signy was breathing hard, perhaps too much to speak, but she didn't show fear or try to send him away. She turned a corner, running down an alley that dead ended in a thick stand of trees.

Of course. Even if she was human, she had a bear's blood. If Otto had frightened her, she would seek refuge in the nearest thing she could reach to a forest. She clearly had the strength to keep running at least that far, whether it was fear or her father's legacy that gave it to her.

"Yes, ma'am," Kai said. He fell back a couple of paces to let her lead, looking around to see if anyone was watching.

No one seemed to be paying them any attention, and soon they were in among the trees. Kai tugged his sunglasses off as he entered the comparative darkness under the trees' canopy.

Princess Signy ran until she reached a blacktop path among the trees, and then she stopped and turned to face Kai. He could see her moving to plant herself there just as she had on the sidewalk, facing Otto, but as soon as their eyes met, Kai lost his breath and all other thoughts.

His lion roared as Kai stared into the princess's dark brown eyes. The recognition struck him like lightning.

My mate. She is my mate. She stood facing him with her lush pink lips parted, her cheeks brightly flushed from her run. Her dark hair was falling down in wisps around her face, and he could almost feel the heat of her body as he stepped closer. Her full breasts rose and fell rapidly with her breath, and he knew just how much strength underlay the soft curves of her body.

She was meant for him, made for him, for all that he'd had to come to this far-off place to find her. He was already sworn to protect her as a princess of Valtyra, but the need for his mate, this woman before him, went deeper than any oath, any words. This was not just duty or loyalty. In the blink of an eye, he had fallen in love.

"Kai?" Princess Signy raised a hand toward him, and Kai realized suddenly that she was looking at him as if she felt it too. It was rare for a human to know her mate when she saw him. But then, Princess Signy was no ordinary human.

She was also much more than just Kai's mate. With an effort, he mastered the urge to take her outstretched hand. Instead, he clasped his hands behind his back in a hard grip. "Your Highness."

She frowned, shaking her head slightly. "Kai—what—what is this? As soon as I met your eyes, I... I feel like I..." She hesitated, choosing a word. "I *know* you."

No one had told her what it meant, any more than they had told her about any other part of her heritage. Kai looked down, trying to remember when it had been explained to him. Had it ever been? All he could think of was his father explaining why his mother had gone away, why he was to have a new mother now, and he couldn't stand to think of that with his own mate standing before him.

"Many of us—Valtyrans of the clans—we have a way of knowing when we meet the right one for us. We call that one our *mate*. I think you are mine, and if you feel it too, then I think I am yours."

He took a step closer, wanting to reach out. He could feel his lion inside, restless as if it were pacing a cage, needing to be near her, to protect her.

But he had to go carefully. There were some things that claws and teeth and strength couldn't protect her from.

"Princess," he said softly, still not quite daring to use her first name without permission. "What did Otto say to you? What made you run from him?"

Signy sniffed, folding her arms—Kai didn't let himself look at the way the motion pressed her breasts together—and shook her head. Her eyes held a stubborn glint when she looked at Kai. "He didn't *scare* me, if that's what you're thinking. He just—he said something that made me remember my father, and..."

Signy looked away again, her shoulders sagging a little. "I thought I didn't remember him at all. I thought I'd made up stories about him when I was little, fantasies, like an imaginary friend. But I realized that what I remember was real, and then I just... I missed him so much at that moment, I couldn't..."

Her voice was shaking. Kai stepped cautiously forward.

It was no wonder if she was feeling unstrung by all of

this. Hearing the truth of Valtyra and her place in it would be many shocks at once. And to stir up grief on top of it would be too much for anyone. Kai had certainly encountered plenty of young women, and young men for that matter, who would have been screaming by now, lashing out or falling to pieces.

Signy just hadn't wanted to let an arrogant stranger see her cry.

"I'm sorry," Kai said quietly. "For your loss. If you—if you wish privacy, Princess..."

She shook her head hard but didn't turn to face him. "Could you... could you call me by my name? Please?"

"Signy."

She turned all at once. Kai's arms were already open for her, and he wrapped them around her, bringing her close. She hid her face against his shoulder, and he smoothed his hand over her hair, finding the clips that held it in place and freeing them. Her hair fell down in a dark cascade. Signy sighed and leaned into him, welcoming the release.

Kai breathed in the warm womanly scent of her and tried not to notice too much how good it felt to have her soft body pressed so tightly to his. He could feel her taking quick, deep breaths, but she barely made a sound.

After a few moments she stepped back, wiping a few stray tears from her cheeks with quick brushes of her fingers. She took a breath and smiled up at him, looking wondering. "Still, I guess... I found you. So that's—that's not all bad, right? If... If I come to Valtyra, we can be together."

Kai gave her a crooked smile and raised one hand in a gesture of *maybe, maybe not.*

"It's complicated. Your Highness."

Signy frowned. "But you said... You said it's a Valtyran thing, to know who's right for you. If we both know..."

Kai swallowed. "How much did Otto tell you about what's expected of you," he forced the word out, the same one she had used, "*if* you come to Valtyra?"

19

Signy's gaze sharpened in thought, and Kai caught a startling glimpse of her resemblance to the king. Not the frail man Kai had been guarding these last five years, but as he had been in his prime, canny and thoughtful.

"He told me I can't rule, because I'm human," Signy said slowly. "But my grandfather has no other heir, so..."

She trailed off, her gaze rising to meet hers. He watched her stunned expression as she worked it out, and said the words so she wouldn't have to.

"You must marry a shifter, and soon. Because the man who marries the Princess of Valtyra will be our next king."

3

SIGNY

Like a lot of things Signy had heard in the past hour, it should have sounded ridiculous and instead it was utterly serious.

Kai, big and strong and solid, golden and gorgeous and somehow, miraculously, meant just for her, was looking her squarely in the eyes. He said it like he was telling her that the medication she needed to take had an unfortunate unpredictable side effect of *sudden death*.

After a moment, Signy pulled herself together enough to say, "So that's... not a plus for you, then?"

Kai looked startled by his own smile, but the warmth of it steadied her. She wasn't alone in feeling this pull, this strange rightness. He shared it with her. They recognized the same thing in each other. There had to be a way to work out the rest.

"I'm not arrogant enough to say I would be the best man for the job," Kai said. "But I know enough to know that I wouldn't be the worst who could take it on. When you stand as close to the king as I have for five years now, as a guardsman, you see what goes into running the kingdom."

Complicated, Kai had said. It wasn't just that he didn't want to take on the task of becoming a prince, and then a king, in order to be with her. It was that he might not be allowed to. Because he was a mere guard? Or...

Signy thought of Otto, that briefcase full of papers. She wondered what else he would have handed over to her, already signed and settled, if she hadn't run away from him.

"Have I been betrothed to someone I never met since I was a baby?" Signy guessed. "Some... some alliance or something?"

Kai's eyebrows rose, and he smiled again. "No, or not formally, not that I ever heard of. But as the Princess Royal, you'll need the king's permission to marry—and the king will be advised in his decision by his Council. I can claim no family or connections to influence them."

"But Otto's probably got a dozen wolves lined up for me, huh?" Signy wrinkled her nose at the thought of a younger version of Otto, coolly ambitious. By definition, the only men who might marry her were the ones who would throw away their chance at a true mate to do it. "But there has to be a way, Kai."

Kai nodded. "I think the king will listen. Even if you don't know him well, he is your grandfather. He has always regretted that your father and you were estranged from him, and that he never had grandchildren who grew up in Valtyra, for him to see. The queen was his true mate, and he married her despite the advantage a different bride might have brought him—she was a bird shifter, not of noble family. If we can speak to him directly, without the council's interference, and make him understand, then we'll have a chance."

"But the council is going to interfere," Signy interpreted. "Otto, is he..."

"Your grandfather is old, and his health is not the best," Kai said, hesitating over his words.

Signy was reminded of the careful way the pharmacists spoke sometimes, carefully not contradicting a customer's doctor or overstepping what they were allowed to say in the way of medical advice.

"He relies very heavily on his council, especially on the First Minister. And as a member of the Royal Guard, I must also have the king's permission to marry, because it will mean laying down my duties as a guardsman. The Royal Guard is forbidden from interfering in politics, so if this is seen as ambition on my part rather than an honest match... refusing his permission is the least of what the king might do."

Signy's eyes went wide at the matter-of-fact tone in Kai's voice. "Are you saying... Asking permission to marry me could be a crime? What would happen to you?"

"I could be cast out of the guard and exiled, or conscripted into military service overseas, or... well. I doubt it would come to that."

Signy shook her head. This wasn't just a strange fairy tale she'd fallen into, complete with a stunningly gorgeous hero of her very own. Kai could be in real danger. For that matter, if she didn't cooperate with these people, what would happen to her? Would they decide to just dispose of a princess who didn't want to marry whoever they told her to? She was only *human*, after all.

Kai stepped closer, setting his hands on her arms. "I can't tell you there's nothing to be frightened of, Signy. But I will protect you to my last breath, and all the Royal Guard is sworn to do the same."

Signy pulled away, taking a few fast steps down the path, deeper into the park. She hadn't signed up for this. She wasn't supposed to be responsible for people possibly getting *killed*. She didn't know the first thing about being a princess.

"Can't we just—" Signy looked back toward Kai, and somehow wasn't surprised that he was only a half-step behind her. "Just forget all of that? You could stay here, or we could go away somewhere together—we could just forget all about Valtyra!"

Kai looked like she'd punched him. Signy covered her mouth like she'd said something horrible, even though she wasn't sure what was so bad. It had obviously hurt Kai, and the stricken look on his face made her own heart ache horribly.

I've only known you five minutes, Signy thought. She felt dizzy with secondhand pain and realization. *How do I already love you enough to hurt when you're hurting?*

"Valtyra is my home," Kai said haltingly. "All my life, I have loved it, and I—I would wish to share it with you. To show you." He swallowed, and went on more strongly. "And if we went away, the problem would remain there— no heir to the throne, and the king and council left to choose his successor. It could get... very messy, and the treaties that keep Valtyra's secrets from being known by the whole human world could be at risk. All our people would be in danger."

Signy bit her lip, feeling like a selfish child. She thought of the grandfather she'd never met, frail and old, all his family gone except her. Could she leave him to be manipulated by Otto and God knew who else? There had to be a way she could make this work. She and Kai, together, had to be able to do this.

"Signy," Kai said, just a whisper. She met his eyes again.

They were a brilliant amber color, with too much gold in them to be called brown, and just now they were so intent they almost glowed. The hurt was still there in his eyes, but she could see him squaring himself against it. "If you can't come to Valtyra..."

Signy shook her head quickly, stepping in and reaching up to touch his face. "I won't make you desert the king, and your home. We'll find a way. There must be a way."

He exhaled, his eyes slipping closed, and Signy couldn't resist any longer. She went up on her tiptoes, giving him a kiss to seal her promise.

A shocking bolt of heat went through her at the touch of Kai's lips. *Mine,* she thought, *my mate, you are mine.*

Kai made a low rough sound that was almost a growl. His arms went around her, crushing her close. She clung to him as the kiss deepened, turning from a promise to a proposition. *Yes, yes, darling, yes.*

Kai pulled back from her all at once. In the silence as they stared at each other, gazes locked, she heard a faint electronic chirp.

Kai squeezed his eyes shut and stepped back, pulling out his phone. "Yes? Yes. I'm with the princess."

Except that wasn't exactly what he was saying, Signy realized, watching the motion of his kiss-reddened lips. He was speaking another language—Valtyran? And she understood it as clearly as if he were speaking English.

"She's fine, she only needed a moment to collect her thoughts," Kai said, switching into English and looking up to meet her eyes. "I shouldn't speak for her beyond that— Your Highness? It's Count Sparre af Varg."

Signy took a deep breath to compose herself, remembering that she had to keep quiet about what had just passed between her and Kai. They would have to keep the secret all the way back to Valtyra somehow.

She took Kai's phone, stepping close enough to him so that he could still hear. "Yes? This is Signy."

"Your Highness," Otto said. "I apologize for giving you such a shock earlier. I will leave the papers with your guard, Tristan, so that you may examine them at your leisure."

Signy looked up, meeting Kai's gaze. He looked as surprised as she was. "Leave? Are you going somewhere?"

"I must return to Valtyra," he said briskly. "The king is not well, and I am needed there. I shall prepare everything for your arrival, and you may follow in your own time—a jet from the royal fleet awaits you at the airport. Your guards will see to your safety and assist you with all you need in the meantime."

Signy's jaw dropped. She looked up at Kai, eyes wide as she wondered what on earth to do about this. She had a feeling it couldn't be good, no matter how relieved she would be to have Otto out of the way.

After all, he would be going straight back to her grandfather—and no doubt lobbying for his own choice for who should marry Signy. If she gave him enough time she might step off a plane and straight into her own wedding to some stranger!

"I could come with you," Signy said quickly. "I'll just pack a few things, then we can all travel together."

There was a pause from Otto, and then a chuckle that made Signy feel dirty even before he spoke. "Well, I suppose anyone would be eager to be a princess, hm? Still, there is no need for unseemly haste, my dear—sleep on your decision, take some time to consider what you're choosing and tie up your affairs here."

Signy wanted to snarl at that *my dear*, but she let it go for now. "I was thinking that if my grandfather is so ill, I should hurry to meet him while there's still time."

"No, no," Otto said smoothly. "The king's health is not so precarious as that; it is just that running the kingdom without assistance is a strain for him. When you come, if you will take your time, we can clear his schedule so that his time is free to spend with you."

Signy looked up at Kai, whose face was a mask of restraint. "Well, I look forward to seeing him as soon as I can," Signy said. "We have so much to catch up on." It occurred to her that *she* was supposed to be the princess here, so she added, "Thank you for letting me know, Otto. Goodbye."

There was a little pause. Kai's eyes widened, but his lips twitched up in an almost-smile. Otto said stiffly, "Goodbye, Your Highness."

Signy handed the phone back to Kai, and he hung it up and said, "You did well, Princess. Otto is formidable, and there is no easy way to get around him."

Signy leaned into Kai and he wrapped his arm around her while tapping buttons on his phone.

"Magnus," he said, and then a stream of quick Valtyran. She only understood a handful of words this time; Kai was talking faster than before. But she could *almost* understand it, like hearing faint snatches of a song she knew she would recognize if she could just hear more of it.

Kai hung up the phone and squeezed her closer against his side. "How soon do you wish to travel, Princess?"

"Tomorrow," Signy said decisively. "I don't care if that's unseemly—I can pack and sleep on it and go."

Kai nodded, turning her back the way they had come. Signy went willingly, eager to *do something* about all of this as soon as she could.

~~*

Signy thought about her mother as she quickly and efficiently packed up a suitcase and backpack. She had learned to pack up and go like this from her mother; they had moved again and again when Signy was young. Her dad— stepfather—had been just as free-spirited, forever looking for some new opportunity. They'd lived in a half a dozen different co-ops, out-of-season vacation homes, tents and trailers and the occasional motel.

Signy had finally had to put her foot down and stay behind in order to finish her entire senior year at the same high school. Her parents hadn't been concerned about her going to college, any more than they were concerned about Poppy's backpacking year extending indefinitely. It was more important to be a *student of the world*, her mother insisted. But Signy had always wanted to stay somewhere, to have roots, a home she could come back to always.

She had never really wondered what made her mother that way; she always thought it was just how she was. But now, thinking of her mother's signature on Signy's ornate royal birth certificate, remembering the way she felt when she met Kai's gaze for the first time, she wondered if it wasn't something else.

Had her mother felt this way about her father? They had lived in one place for Signy's whole life until he died, and he had been a police officer in his adopted city. He had obviously wanted to stay, to help people—*protect and serve*—and Signy's mother had stayed put too.

But then came the accident and her father's death. Signy's mother had lost her mate and her anchor all at once.

Signy glanced up from her packing to find Kai watching her.

"If you need to bring more..."

Signy shook her head, wondering what she would do if she lost him. Could she bear to stay in Valtyra without him? Would she drift across the world like her mother and sister, never content, never at home again?

"I travel light," Signy said, zipping her suitcase shut and pushing it over to him. She swung her backpack onto her own shoulder. "Shall we?"

He still hesitated. "Are there... people you need to say goodbye to? Of course you'll be able to travel, visit, but..."

Signy shook her head. "None of my family lives here, and I just started my job yesterday. I don't think they'll be that surprised if I just never come back."

Kai raised his eyebrows in question at that, and Signy dug her hated nametag out of her pocket to show him. He grimaced at it and tossed it into the trash can. "Very well, Your Highness. Shall we?"

Signy nodded and followed him out.

The black-haired guard was waiting for them down in the sleek car—Otto must have called a cab to the airport. Kai had introduced him earlier as Tristan, and he had only nodded briefly, murmuring, "Your Highness."

Now Signy sat in the back seat alone and Kai slid in up

front next to Tristan, leaving her alone for the drive downtown to their hotel.

Signy took the opportunity to send a group text to her mother and Poppy. She mulled over the wording for a while, but in the end she decided to be honest.

Met a great guy. Leaving soon to travel to Europe with him. Excited and nervous!!

Poppy didn't respond, but after a few minutes Signy got a text back from her mother's number. *Happy for you hon! Mom is at silent weaving retreat, will let her know when she gets home. Send pics soon! Love, Dad.*

So even if she wanted to, Signy couldn't call her mother and ask for advice, or ask whether she had felt like this about Signy's father. Her mother would probably tell her that was a sign, or to follow her heart.

Signy hung up her phone and tucked it away. A moment later the car pulled to a stop in front of one of the fanciest hotels downtown. Dark had finally fallen, but it was bright as day under the lights of the hotel sign. Kai was out of the car and opening her door before the hotel's doorman could reach her. Signy smiled apologetically and let herself be herded inside.

Kai ushered her across the marble-floored lobby, hushed with thick carpets under the fine furniture of the seating area, straight to the elevators.

Signy looked back toward the door. "Tristan...?"

"He'll handle the car and bring in your luggage," Kai said, pressing a button as the elevator's doors closed smoothly on them. Signy was faintly surprised to see herself in the mirror and realize that she was still wearing her work clothes. She looked out of place beside Kai, slightly rumpled in his impeccable dark suit.

But Kai was watching her with heat in his eyes like he wanted to devour her.

She *was* about to spend a night in the fanciest hotel she'd ever stayed in, and there was no one here they had to keep secrets from.

"Oh," Signy whispered. She could feel herself blushing, and it wasn't only her face heating up.

Kai smiled wickedly, and the elevator chimed softly as it came to a stop, the doors sliding back. Kai led her a short way down the hall to a door that opened on a living room, with doors leading to bedrooms open on either side. Among the elegant and old-fashioned furnishings, she saw several wooden trunks stamped with the royal crest. Gold leaf shone on the crown over the yellow aspen trees and shining white bears.

"We took a suite, not knowing how long we might need to stay," Kai explained. "And the ladies in waiting at the palace packed up some things for you. You should have the corner room, there."

Kai gestured to the room on the right, and Signy drifted through, glancing back to find Kai swinging one enormous trunk easily up onto his shoulder. He followed her with it, setting it down under one of the four windows in the room. There was no door direct to the hallway from here, just an enormous bathroom.

There was also an enormous bed. Signy glanced from it to Kai, but she felt suddenly shy—and grimy, after a day's work and that unplanned run through the humid evening.

"I'm just going to... freshen up," Signy said, waving toward the bathroom.

Kai nodded and stepped closer to her, his expression turning serious. "Princess—Signy—it might be wiser for us to keep apart tonight. We will have to hide what we feel when we reach Valtyra, and once we arrive... you will have decisions to make. People don't always marry their mates; it could be that you—"

Signy tugged Kai down into a kiss, cutting off his words, though she had wondered herself if she might have to make a choice like that.

"Only you," she whispered. "I only want you. At least tonight—I'm not a princess yet, and we're not in Valtyra. Please? Let us just be Kai and Signy, who know they're meant to be together. Just tonight, at least."

Kai sighed and kissed her again. "Tonight, at least," he agreed softly. "I'll... tell Tristan something. Go on, I'm sure you could use a moment alone."

Signy shook her head and kissed him one more time, and then made herself turn away, stepping into a bathroom bigger than some bedrooms she'd shared with Poppy. The floor was creamy marble tile, and there was a huge Jacuzzi tub beside the glass-fronted shower, which was nearly as big as the elevator she'd just ridden up in.

She stripped out of her clothes, dropping them in a neat pile on the counter, and stepped into the shower. Water pounded down on her, deliciously hot after the chill of the air-conditioned hotel room. She stood for a while, letting herself be rinsed clean. She tried to think of nothing else, to feel nothing but the water washing over her.

After a while Signy found the soap and shampoo left out for her—beautiful locally made stuff, smelling sweet-spicy, like honey and lavender. She washed twice just for the pleasure of it, then finally shut off the shower. She wrung her hair out and wrapped it up in a fluffy white towel before drying herself with another, then took the time to comb out her hair properly. She ventured cautiously back into the bedroom, but she was alone—though she could see that she had had a visitor.

Her own bags were set at the foot of the bed, on top of one of the trunks she'd seen in the outer room. A second trunk stood open beside that one, showing a riot of brightly colored fabrics carefully packed inside.

One item had already been unpacked for her: a red silk bathrobe was laid out on the bed. The hems and cuffs were richly embroidered with threads of yellow and white—not just aspens and bears, but suns and stars and moons, and a riot of little five-petaled flowers. Signy ran a hand gingerly over the beautiful stitching and found it gloriously soft to the touch.

She picked up the robe and slipped it on, and was

somehow unsurprised to find that it was clearly cut for someone with a very full figure. It wrapped securely around her front and fell nearly to her ankles, but it clung so softly, caressing her skin like liquid, that Signy still felt rather provocatively unclothed in it. She opened the door to the next room cautiously.

Tristan was standing all the way across the room, beside the door to the opposite bedroom, with his arms folded across his chest. Kai stood nearer to her own door, though not close enough to crowd her as she peeked out.

Kai looked toward her as soon as she opened the door, and Signy's breath caught as their eyes met, feeling the connection between them click into place all over again. Heat flashed through her body, and the rightness of it, the sense that she *knew* him, struck her all over again.

"Well, shit," Tristan said, drawing Signy's gaze to him.

He touched his hand to his heart and made a half-bow as he said, "I mean, congratulations on the discovery of your mate, Your Highness, and I wish both of you all the best no matter how much extra work you make for the Royal Guard."

Signy looked at Kai again; he was smiling a little. "Coming from Tristan, that's as good as we're likely to get."

She looked back to Tristan, just in time to see him looking toward Kai. He didn't repeat the hand-on-heart bow, but tapped his fingers lightly against his chest and nodded.

Tristan looked back to Signy and gestured toward some trays set out on the low table between the sofas. "There are refreshments, Your Highness. And I believe I will be of most use to you keeping watch from the far room, unless you require some other duty of me?"

Signy glanced toward Kai again, but he had his eyes turned down, hands clasped behind her back, leaving this up to her.

This was the first time she needed to be a princess. She

needed to give some royal command, or dismissal, to her guardsman.

Signy touched her hand lightly to her heart as she looked back at Tristan. "As you think best, Tristan. Thank you. I'll call for you if I need anything else tonight."

Tristan's lips twitched up slightly, but he bowed again and stepped back through the door to the other room, closing it firmly behind him.

Signy's eyes went immediately to Kai, and this time he was looking back at her, smiling. He had shed the jacket of his suit and his tie, and his collar was now open to show his tanned throat. The sleeves were rolled up to reveal muscular forearms and more tawny golden-tanned skin.

He caught her to him in a tight embrace, and Signy kissed him hungrily. She pulled away only when she had to breathe, and turned her head away to keep from meeting Kai's gaze again. She didn't think she could breathe at all if she did.

Kai loosened his grip, letting her lean against him, and Signy found herself looking at the trays Tristan had pointed out on the table. She was suddenly aware that she had never had dinner after work. In all the excitement she'd completely forgotten to be hungry, but now she was starving.

Signy looked up at Kai, and found him smiling a different smile—not hot and wicked, but warm and fond. Signy smiled back. "I missed dinner, do you mind?"

"Your wish is my command, Princess." Kai stepped back with a half-bow, ushering her toward the nearest sofa. Signy put her chin up and strode past him in as regal a manner as she could summon.

In the next moment she was sinking into the softness of the sofa—not at all the hard, formal piece of furniture she had half expected. She relaxed into the cushions, arranging the luscious folds of her dressing gown around her.

Kai sat down beside her, perching on the edge of the

seat as he picked up the nearest tray and brought it over within her reach in a smooth, practiced motion.

"Do Royal Guards work as waiters, too?" Signy realized that, for all she and Kai had promised each other, they really hardly knew each other.

Kai smiled, turning the tray to let her look at the selection of tidbits offered. "Believe it or not, Valtyra has restaurants, and I had a summer job or two when I was young, before I joined the Royal Guard."

Signy raised her eyebrows, her gaze tracing over his broad shoulders. "As a waiter?"

"Well, no," he admitted, giving her a glimpse of a boyish smile as he ducked his head. "On a fishing boat, one summer, and as a sort of—" he waved his hand. "Park ranger, the next. But it did make me very attentive to people serving me food on my days off, and there were many days when I *wished* for a job as a waiter."

Signy blew out a breath, shaking her head. "I tried the waitressing thing, but I never really got good at flirting for tips—"

Kai made a low rumbling noise that he turned into an unconvincing cough. Signy grinned and pressed her toes against his thigh. "Easy, tiger—"

He actually did growl at that, and Signy ran her eyes over him again. "Oh, not a tiger, huh? No, you're—a lion, aren't you?"

Kai gave her a quick sideways look, and held the tray closer to her. Signy selected a little folded-pastry puff and popped it into her mouth, still watching him and more sure with every passing second that she was right. Quite aside from his golden-tan coloring, his wild blond hair and amber eyes, she could see the self-assured power of a lion in every easy line of his body.

No need to posture and prowl territory like a wolf. Kai knew his strength, and he had the lithe quickness of a cat, not the solidity of a bear.

"I have no right to claim my clan," Kai said carefully.

"For now I am only a lieutenant of the Royal Guard, and I have no other allegiance. But if I took my animal's shape, you would see a very large, maned cat, it is true."

Signy bit her lip and nodded, trying to speak with the appropriate seriousness as she said, "Your secret is safe with me."

It was a little spoiled when she punctuated the words by popping the pastry bite into her mouth and moaned at the flaky richness of it. Kai just smiled and picked up a matching bite for himself and Signy felt vindicated when his eyelids shivered half-shut in pleasure at the taste. They ate in silence for a few minutes, taking turns pointing out promising items to each other, and being only a *little* obvious about licking fingers and lips.

It didn't take long before Signy had eaten enough not to be distractingly hungry anymore, though she still had her eye on a few more things she wanted to try. At the same time, she thought that she might like to go to bed with Kai if he were ready, and it seemed at once so right and so strange to be sure of him, and sure of what she wanted.

"You said this thing with mates, this happens often in Valtyra? My grandfather and grandmother, they were mates? They knew as soon as they met?"

Kai nodded, and picked up a tidbit off the tray, offering it to her. Signy considered eating it from his fingers, but limited herself to letting her hand brush his as she took it from him.

"It's a rather famous story, you'll hear a hundred versions of it," Kai said. "It was summer. The King— Prince Einar, as he was then—was out on a boat, sailing and fishing. A sudden storm came up and capsized his boat, and he changed into his bear shape while the storm lasted, to keep warm in the water. When the storm passed, he wanted to find his boat, and when he reached it he discovered a sparrowhawk perched on it—blown off shore by the storm, looking very bedraggled and tired, but he could tell at once that she was a shifter, and she knew that he was, and she need not be afraid of him. She took wing but circled just above him, and he righted the boat, and then shifted back to his human form—which meant he was naked."

Signy gave a startled little laugh, picturing the view the sparrowhawk—her grandmother!—must have had then.

Kai grinned. "Then she dove down to the water and shifted as well, but on the other side of the boat, so he could only see her face. But that was enough. Their eyes met, and..." Kai gave an elaborate shrug. "Well, they decided that they would not mind sharing the boat after all."

Signy giggled behind her fingers. "Did she... did she know who he was? That he was a prince?"

Kai nodded. "We are a small country, and there are not so many men of the bear kind—even fewer now, but not many then." He looked into her eyes, steady and serious, and she felt her own humor die away. "Are you asking whether she chose him for that?"

Signy shrugged. "I would think that a lot of people would want to say the prince was their mate."

Kai nodded slowly. "Or the princess, perhaps?"

Signy bit her lip. "It's not—I know you—"

Kai shook his head. "It's a good question to ask. But we say in Valtyra, 'what two know is enough'. The prince knew who his mate was, so it didn't matter how many might say that he was theirs. He knew, and she knew, and that was enough."

Kai set the tray aside, so there was nothing between them, and he said softly, "I know what I know, Signy. But what matters is what you know, in your heart."

She knew that Kai hadn't chosen her because he wished to be king. And she knew that she belonged with him, and he with her, whether that meant being royalty in Valtyra or waiting tables in Milwaukee.

"I know," Signy said, reaching out her hand to him.

"We both know. That's enough."

Kai took her hand and kissed it. He pressed his lips to the back, and then her palm, and then in a whirl of motion he swept her up, standing with her in his arms and swinging her around. She clasped her arms around his neck, but she knew she was safe with him, even in that sudden, dizzy whirl.

"Take me to bed, Kai."

"Yes," he murmured, kissing her softly. "Yes, Signy."

He carried her quickly to the bedroom, maneuvering perfectly so that she was never bumped against a wall or a doorframe. He lowered her gently onto the wide, luxurious bed, following her down in a single smooth motion. He stretched out beside her, kissing her, and his hand came to rest on the soft curve of her side.

Only a thin layer of silk separated his hand from her skin. She could feel the heat of his touch through it, and she was sure he must be able to feel the beating of her heart.

Holding his gaze, Signy tugged his hand up to her breast. His thumb stroked her nipple through a fold of silk, and Signy gasped. Kai bent his head and breathed over that spot, then licked, and when he touched her again the wet drag of silk sent heat rushing through her body. She could feel herself getting wet for him.

He sucked softly on her breast through the silk, then raised his head to kiss her again. The next touch of his finger felt like there was nothing between them at all, but Kai murmured against her lips, "Let me see?"

Signy nodded, loosening the tie at her waist that held the robe shut. Kai pushed it back over her shoulder and down her arm, baring her to him.

Signy grabbed a handful of his shirt, already feeling like she had to steady herself against the sensations rushing through her, and Kai had barely touched her yet.

But every touch felt like more than that, as though both their bodies were charged with some secret electricity.

Magic, destiny—whatever it was, it touched her to her core.

Signy watched him as he just stared for a moment. His tongue flicked out to lick his lips as his dark eyes drank her in. Then Kai urged her gently onto her back, bracing himself above her. He kissed her lips again. "Let me do this for you, Signy?"

Signy slipped her fingers into his tawny hair, drawing him down for another kiss. "Yes, Kai, *yes.*"

Kai took control of the kiss and raised one hand to cup her breast, dragging his thumb over the tight, sensitive bud of her nipple. Signy moaned into his mouth, and Kai broke the kiss, dragging his lips down her throat as he moved lower over her. He had both hands on her now, teasing her nipples and caressing her breasts. He kissed over the full curves of them, his lips dragging over her soft skin. Signy whimpered at the sight, getting both her hands into his hair.

"Yes, yes, Kai, oh please—"

His mouth found her nipple, licking hot and wet around the peak. Signy's hips rocked, the sweet pleasure of it gathering heat lower down. When he tested his teeth against the sensitive flesh, Signy gasped, throwing her head back and arching up under him, begging for more.

His hand left her breast, skimming down over her belly.

"Yes?" His breath puffed against kiss-wetted skin.

"Yes, *yes,*" Signy agreed, wriggling her hips and kicking away the puddled silk of the gown. His hand slipped just another inch down, caressing the soft skin of her lower belly, the dark curls of hair there, but not pushing further. Just the promise of what he was doing had her getting wetter, hotter. She tugged his hair, wanting to hide the noises she made against his mouth, wanting his mouth to keep moving lower.

Kai laughed softly against her skin, and Signy giggled herself, knowing that he felt the same impatience and the same joy in what they were doing. He smacked a noisy kiss against her breast and skated his fingers lightly down her belly to her mound. Signy felt the first little tremors of real pleasure from his touch, her belly tightening and her breath speeding.

Kai's fingers slid lower, brushing over her outer folds, barely touching. Signy's hips moved without her volition, begging for more, closer, *deeper*. Kai's mouth touched her again, kissing down the fullness of her belly. She had the feeling, suddenly, that it was no less beautiful to him than the swell of her breasts or the flare of her hips, and she felt breathless in a whole different way.

Then he was nuzzling at the top of the little patch of hair. He looked up at her, his tongue just barely touching her. Signy nodded.

Kai picked his head up and said, "Have you—how slow do I need to go, dearest?"

Signy bit her lip, shrugging a little as she said, "Not—not *that* slow."

He grinned wickedly. "Good. Because we might not have time to go as slowly as you deserved if all of this were new. And this will be better, I promise you."

Signy huffed, nodding. She'd had a few boyfriends before, but sex had never seemed like it was as great as people always said. She'd heard people say it was better when you found the right person, but she'd had no idea it was going to be *this* much better, and they'd barely gotten started. She didn't know if she would survive if the rest was even better.

Kai's fingers stroked her, slipping just barely between her slick folds, and Signy forgot everyone else who had ever touched her. She forgot everything in the world but this: Kai, her lion, her mate, driving her to the edge of losing her mind with just the touch of his hand. He lingered there, teasing her with touches and barely-there brushes of lips, until Signy was soaking wet and panting.

He moved then, gently guiding her to spread her legs wide so that he could settle between them. Signy was aware for a moment that he was still fully clothed. She wanted to see him, touch him, but she was already drowning in the pleasure he was giving to her, and when he knelt between her legs again, she couldn't think of anything else.

Kai bent low over her, and Signy felt a throb of heat between her legs, more wetness pulsing forth. He nuzzled at her for a moment, and she knew he was breathing her in, the scent of his mate. Then he licked, and Signy shook with pleasure, spiraling higher and higher with every touch that followed.

His mouth drove her wild as his fingers dipped inside of her, finding the secret places that made her moan and gasp his name. The sensations built until she was aware of nothing else, just the pounding of her heart and the rhythm of his tongue and fingers.

She tipped over the edge into an explosion of bliss, crying out softly as he stroked her through it, making the climax last until she was panting and trembling.

Finally he moved up over her, kissing her with sticky lips. His big warm body was an anchor as she came down from that peak.

After a while she realized that she could feel his cock pressing against her thigh—he was still hard, and still wearing those elegant black suit trousers.

"Your turn," Signy murmured, nuzzling into a kiss. Kai returned it softly, though she knew he had to be aching for more.

He blew out a breath. "Condom?"

Signy's eyes went wide, startled, and Kai kissed her quickly, shaking his head. "We have to be careful, dearest. Just for now."

"Kai," she whispered. "Kai, you're my mate." *I love you,* she wanted to say, but she knew it had to be too soon for that. "I can't do this with anyone else, not now that I know you."

"I know," Kai murmured. "I won't give you up, Signy.

I won't, I swear. But we will have to be a little—political. And I don't dare have you with nothing between us, not yet."

Signy exhaled and nodded. "I saw some in the bathroom, in the little basket."

Kai kissed her again and then rolled off the bed. He moved with lithe, feline grace as he walked to the bathroom. Signy lay on the bed, enjoying the view—and her smile only widened when he reappeared with a trio of little foil packets in his hand.

He grinned at her, something a little fierce in the way he showed his teeth, and dropped them on the nightstand.

"Guess I have some things to take off before I can put that on, don't I?"

Signy nodded, folding her arms behind her head and sprawling out at ease. "This I want to see."

Kai groaned, but he was smiling as he bent down to kiss her, and he tucked one of the condoms into her hand at the same time.

He undressed quickly. He wasn't trying to make a show of it, but Signy delighted in every new inch of skin he bared for her. He was all golden tan skin and lean muscle. There was only a dusting of blond hair on his chest, but a darker thatch came into view when he opened his pants. When he peeled them down, his erection stood up from a nest of dark blond curls, thick and hard. Signy wanted every inch at the same time she knew she'd never had anything as big as that inside her—but she felt herself getting wet again, needing more, and she sat up on the bed to coax him closer.

He reached out his hand for the condom she was still holding, but Signy shook her head, scooting to the edge of the bed and reaching for him. She closed her hand around the shaft, fascinated by the silkiness over that hard core, and Kai's breath caught.

She looked up at him. Kai was actually trembling a little with the effort of keeping still, letting her look and touch her fill. She grinned and leaned closer, flicking out her tongue to taste him as he'd tasted her. He tasted sharper, almost bitter, but she found that even without a shifter's senses, she loved the scent of her mate. She breathed him in, tasting again and again before Kai groaned and pushed her back on the bed, following her down to kiss her mouth.

She could feel his bare hardness, hot against her belly, and she was still holding the condom. She broke the kiss and tore it open, and Kai plucked it from her fingers and rolled it on. His fingers kept moving without pause, sliding inside her, but Signy was so wet and so eager that they sank in easily.

"Your turn," Signy whispered, raising one leg to hook over his hip, urging him closer.

Kai groaned again, but a moment later the stroking of his fingers was replaced by the thick head of his erection, and he was pushing slowly into her. Signy gasped at the delicious hot stretch as he filled her, inch by inch, sinking deeper as he kissed her again and again. He felt so perfect inside her, exactly what she had always needed and never known. Her mate.

"Yes, yes," she gasped when he was fully sheathed inside her. Then Kai began to move. Just rocking his hips first, and then moving in slow rolling thrusts, his hardness stroking into her again and again, steady as the tide. Signy didn't even realize how her own pleasure was being stoked again until she was close to coming again. Her whole body felt electrified as she gasped and arched up to meet Kai's thrusts.

His thumb teased her nipple as he kept moving inside her, and Signy went off like a firework, a wild burst of pleasure overtaking her.

She felt Kai still moving inside her, through the waves of her climax, until he groaned with a last, hard thrust into her and went still, and she knew he was coming inside her. She stroked her fingers through his hair as the delirious

42

height of pleasure ebbed.

After a moment he kissed her again, soft and drowsy now.

"Mine," he said softly. "My mate."

"Yours," Signy agreed, cuddling into him. "As you are mine."

4

KAI

Kai woke up with a smile on his face. He could swear his lion was purring, lounging contentedly inside him.

His mate was in his arms. She had promised herself to him, and nothing could separate them. Kai buried his face in the tumbled dark silk of Signy's hair, cuddling her closer. He'd never known it would feel like this, like all was right with the world and nothing else mattered.

This must be how my father felt when—

Kai cut off the thought, but it was too late to stop the awareness, like a dash of cold water. *This* was what it felt like to find your mate, knowing that marrying her might be impossible, or simply disastrous.

Kai eased away from Signy to look up at the ceiling. He felt things rearrange in his mind, like the earth shifting under his feet. He had always known that his parents weren't mates, but it wasn't until he was nine years old that that fact became something more.

That was when his mother had come into his playroom and told him she had to go away for a while, and then never returned. She had written letters on and off for a few years, but even those had dwindled to nothing before too long.

His father had sat him down and explained: his father *did* have a mate, but he hadn't met her until after he married Kai's mother, who was a perfect countess and lioness to help him with the work of leading the af Leijona clan.

We liked each other well enough—that was love, I thought. And then I met my mate, and when I told your mother about it, she revealed that she had already met hers some time before.

Kai had soon gained a human stepmother, and the following year his half-sister Laila had been born. He had not been able to blame a baby for the loss of his own mother, but he had never forgiven his stepmother, or his father. His father had tried to be fair, but Kai had never stopped being aware that he was the child of the woman who *wasn't* his father's mate, who he hadn't loved.

His mother had left him without a backward look for her mate, all but erasing herself from Kai's life, but his father and stepmother had been right there to take all of Kai's blame.

Kai had grown further apart from his father as he grew up. As soon as he had the freedom to he spent less and less time at home, working menial summer jobs to stay away from them.

When his father gently suggested that marrying a woman who wasn't his mate might be his duty, as the next Count and head of the clan, Kai had joined the Royal Guard rather than risk having that conversation again.

Of course, that had not stopped his baby sister, Laila, from following him. For the past year she had worked for the royal household, in the palace. They couldn't claim one another as brother and sister, but Kai hadn't been able to resist liking her, becoming friendly with her all over again as an adult. Their parents' actions weren't any more Laila's fault than Kai's, after all.

They never mentioned their mothers to each other, though, never spoke of mates or marriage.

And now, here was Kai, repeating his father's history all out of order. He had found his mate, and she was human and a thousand times more dangerous to him than a beautiful clerk from the chancellor's office had been to his father.

But Signy is mine, Kai thought, his lion growling inside in affirmation. He could never let her go, never fail to protect her.

He had sworn an oath to protect the crown of Valtyra and its royal family. Could he really do what was best for Signy? Could he protect her in the ways she truly needed to be protected, while letting his lion lead him around?

If Signy concluded that it was best—for her, for the kingdom—to take some other spouse, despite the love they shared, despite their bond...

Kai squeezed his eyes shut and pushed the thought away. They would speak privately to the king. He would surely understand, and he would give his blessing to the match. Kai would be able to marry Signy, properly, honorably.

And then, for the sake of keeping and protecting his mate, he would have to become *King of Valtyra.*

Kai's eyes flashed open again, but this time he found that Signy was looking back at him, blinking sleepily. She gave him a drowsy smile, and all apprehension dissolved in the heat of certainty. She was his mate. He would do whatever he had to do to keep her. He leaned in to kiss the sweet curve of her mouth.

They jerked apart at a thunderous pounding at the door. "Breakfast," Tristan called out. "Time to get a move on."

Kai met Signy's eyes again, watching warily for her reaction to this reminder of the real world.

Signy looked back, her lips twitching. After a moment, she lost the fight for self-control and began to laugh. Kai laughed too, in relief and renewed love for his impossible princess.

Tristan had to pound on the door again before they managed to get up and out of bed, still giggling.

~~*

Signy's reaction to Tristan's poor performance as a royal house servant turned out to be a fair sign of her reaction to everything else. She sat down to study all the papers Otto had left, including Signy's Valtyran passport, and she was charmed and delighted by the gold leaf decorating the little red leather booklet.

Kai felt his lion strutting inside, taking all credit for his mate's happiness. Logically, he knew that he had almost nothing to do with it. But then Signy would look over at him and her smile would turn into something private, something just for him, and he had to resist kissing her again, holding her.

They really weren't going to be able to keep this a secret for long.

He tried to control himself once they had packed up and left the hotel, Signy wearing a lightweight silk dress she had found in one of the trunks the women of the household had packed up for her. He kept a mask of professionalism in place as they packed up all the luggage, loading it into a car; he volunteered to drive the luggage while Tristan brought Signy to the airport in another car.

She gave him a single searching look. Then she nodded slightly, assuring him that she understood. He touched his hand to his heart and bowed to her, as he would to any member of the royal family.

No one had ever made his heart ache this way as he did it, as if he needed to keep his hand pressed there so that it wouldn't overflow, or crack in half.

He told himself it would be a relief to be apart from her for a little while and have nothing to hide, but his lion stalked back and forth all the while. It was all but roaring within him with the need to be near his mate again.

He distracted himself by calling Magnus to report in.

"Kai? Some change from Tristan's report an hour ago?"

Kai opened and closed his mouth. Magnus sounded harried. Whatever Otto had been up to since returning, it couldn't have been good. "No, sir."

"Then we'll see you tonight," Magnus said. There was nothing in his voice to indicate whether Tristan had told Kai's secret.

"Yes, sir," Kai replied, the only possible answer, and Magnus was gone again.

Kai felt more unsettled than he had before he called. After a moment's thought he dialed another number.

"Kai!" His sister's voice brought an instant smile to his face. "Tell me what's going on immediately, everything has been madness here since Otto got in last night. He's been closeted with the king for hours, along with the master of ceremonies and Lady Teresa, and word is they're planning all sorts of events that we ought to have had a *year's* warning for—"

Kai laughed at Laila's frazzled rush of words, even though he also knew that this was serious. Otto had the king's ear again, and he was orchestrating God knew what for Signy. That was his way—he would do everything quietly, behind closed doors, giving them nothing to fight back against.

"We found the princess," Kai said. "Signy is—" Kai caught himself speaking familiarly of the princess and cut himself off from saying more. "She's very friendly. American, you know. You'll like her, she's wonderful. And we're leaving within the hour to come back to Valtyra. We'll be there tonight."

"*Tonight!*" Laila shrieked. "Kai! There's so much to *do*! Her rooms aren't nearly ready, and we'll have to prepare—oh, I must fly! Thank you!"

Laila hung up, even more abruptly than Magnus had, but Kai found himself smiling, imagining the eager flurry of preparations she would set in motion. His princess would be well provided for once they arrived, at least. He had done that much for her.

He was soon at the airport, presenting his paperwork and being directed to the royal jet. The jet's crew met him on the tarmac and helped him to load everything, and a moment later Tristan pulled up and handed Signy out.

She gave the plane a beaming, rapturous look, and Kai looked away to hide his own answering smile. Not in front of the crew; there was no knowing which of them might say something to Otto or to someone who would report to him.

When Kai dared to look back at Signy again, she was standing very still with her shoulders straight, only a polite smile on her face. Tristan introduced her to the pilot, and Signy nodded, smiled, and offered her hand to shake.

Kai focused on loading up her trunks, and didn't so much as look toward her.

He was already on board when she stepped onto the plane, so he got to see the look of wonder come over her face again at the luxurious appointments. The pilot guided her through the front lounge area, showing her the private bedroom and bathroom at the rear, for her exclusive use.

Kai stared out the window as he listened to her *ooh* and *ahh*, and did not picture her sitting—lying—on the wide royal bed in that pretty silk dress, the hem riding up past her knees to give a glimpse of her thighs...

A hard punch on his arm brought his eyes open again. Tristan was giving him a stern look, but there was a hint of amusement lurking at the corner of his mouth.

Kai exhaled and nodded, raising one hand to rub his arm. He had to stay focused. He had a job to do here, and doing it perfectly was the only way he could help Signy now.

The pilot left Signy to enjoy her private space on the plane and came forward again, nodding briefly to Kai and Tristan before he went up to the cockpit. Kai looked around the plane again, wondering how he could occupy himself for the next several hours. He couldn't go near Signy, and she didn't really need guarding from anything aboard the plane.

His phone vibrated in his pocket. Kai pulled it out and saw it was Laila calling. He frowned and glanced toward Tristan, who stepped in closer as Kai accepted the call. "Laila?"

"Her Highness is American, correct?" Laila asked briskly. "Born there, raised there?"

"Correct," Kai said, glancing in the direction Signy had gone.

"So she'll need some training," Laila said. "How to conduct herself correctly, royal etiquette, who's who. In order to avoid embarrassing herself, or looking like too much like a foreigner, or—she'll need to learn things."

"Yes," Kai agreed. "That's why we're coming to Valtyra right away, so she can start at once."

Laila made a tiny, frustrated noise. "Well, someone should have told the king's council that, because they're going to be greeting her publicly when she arrives."

Kai felt suddenly cold inside; in his sister's exasperated voice he could hear the echo of things the guards barely dared to discuss among themselves. He could see Otto's hand in this, all too clearly. Once again, he had maneuvered so that there was nothing to accuse him of, nothing to fight back against.

"What do you mean by publicly?"

"I mean people are *already* assembling at the airfield. It's going to be a mob by the time Her Highness arrives. Half the kingdom will be watching everything she does from the moment she sets foot in Valtyra, and she can't possibly be ready for that."

Any mistakes she made would be seen instantly, known by everyone. They would make it easier for Otto to claim the princess didn't know what she was doing, that she was an American who had no idea how to conduct herself in

Valtyra and couldn't be trusted to choose her own spouse. It would be an excuse for the council to control her, to undermine her ability to speak for herself.

"We've got eight hours," Kai said, turning toward the door to the royal chamber. "Did you send the right things for her to wear? Who can coach her on protocol over the phone?"

"I don't know, we're all rushing around—"

"The royal household serves the royal family," Kai said, a little sharply. "That includes the princess. We have to find someone. What about one of the retired ladies in waiting? Is Margrethe in Bjornholm?"

"Right," Laila said. "I'll see. Tell Her Highness?"

"I will. And—thank you, Laila."

"We serve the royal family," Laila parroted back, and hung up again.

Kai knocked on Signy's door. She opened it a few seconds later, giving him a melting smile that turned to confusion as she saw his expression—and Tristan flanking him.

"I'm afraid we're taking you into an ambush," Kai said briskly. "We need you to be ready to be Her Royal Highness Princess Signy as soon as you walk off the plane."

Signy's lips tightened. "Otto?"

Kai nodded, feeling a rush of pride at Signy's quick perception. "A public welcome for you. One of the royal household's ladies, Laila, is working to find someone who can brief you on all the correct protocol, and probably what to wear, but I thought you should know as soon as possible."

The PA clicked on above them, and the pilot said, "Your Highness, gentlemen, please prepare for takeoff."

Signy waved them inside and went to sit down in an armchair that was secured as firmly as any standard seat. Kai took a seat on a plainer bench, and Tristan sat down beside him. He watched Signy's face as the plane accelerated down the runway, studying her expression as she thought about what he'd told her.

Would it be too much? Would she want to run away again? If she did, was it his duty to go with her, or convince her to stay?

The plane lifted into the air and Signy let out a breath, tipping her head back. Kai glanced over at Tristan, but he was watching the princess intently, and Kai had to look again as well, to see what Tristan was seeing.

What Kai saw then was her profile. It was startling to realize how familiar it was. He had known that she favored her father and the royal family, but with her eyes closed and her head turned, he could see suddenly that Signy was truly a princess and future queen. Her profile belonged on coins, her portrait should—would—hang in the royal galleries.

Still Signy was motionless, saying nothing, until the pilot announced, "Your Highness, gentlemen, you may now move freely around the plane."

Signy picked her head up, looking straight at Kai. "All right. Tell me what I need to know. Who's going to be at this public welcome? What do I call them?"

Kai grinned, looking over at Tristan, who pointed to a small desk in the corner. "Your Highness has a laptop available, if I may?"

Signy nodded, and Tristan went to fetch the laptop.

"It will be the royal council," Kai explained. "We can go over pictures of each of them, so you'll recognize them."

Signy nodded decidedly as Tristan brought the computer over and sat down in the next armchair, searching for pictures.

"I'll need to know their families, too," Signy said. "I mean—their clans, their alliances, right? Who's with Otto, who might be willing to listen to me."

Tristan shot Kai a look. They were both from old families, though they had both vowed to forget their

53

families in service to the crown. They were not to meddle in politics. And yet, Signy had to know what anyone in the palace would know.

Kai was up to his neck in this anyway. "I'll tell you those parts," he said. "Tristan—"

"No, I'll help," Tristan said. "As Her Highness commands, I cannot do otherwise."

Kai felt a rush of gratitude for his friend and fellow guard's support, and Signy nodded firmly. "Right, then. I guess the first thing I have to learn is Otto, right? He's First Minister? What do I call him?"

"Your Grace," Kai offered, coming over to perch on the edge of Signy's bed. "And he should bow to you when he greets you; you stand still until he's reached the full depth of the bow, then—like this—" Kai showed the little hand gesture. "You release him."

~~*

Lady Margrethe, a white-haired dowager of the king's generation, called a little later to review protocol with Signy. However, that didn't release Kai and Tristan from their work helping Signy prepare.

There were bows and salutes to demonstrate and practice, and Signy had to learn the curtsey she would give when presented to the king, though no one thought that His Majesty would be present when she stepped off the plane. It was not proper for the king to wait upon his granddaughter, even if he had been in better health.

Eventually Margrethe—having switched to a video call on the laptop—announced that Her Highness needed to rest, and ejected Kai and Tristan from the room with an air of perfect aristocratic confidence. They were both outside before Kai had a chance to think about resisting, or trying to steal a moment or a word alone with Signy.

Tristan gave him a long look and shook his head. "You should lie down too. I don't think you're going to get much sleep in Bjornholm."

Kai wanted to argue, but Tristan had a point. He stretched out on the thick carpet in the plane's lounge room while Tristan settled at a desk to work on a report.

His lion was restless, but Kai assured himself, lion and man both, that Signy was in good hands, and well on her way to being properly prepared. He would have to be alert for trouble when they arrived, and that meant being well-rested.

Somehow, he slept.

When he woke, Tristan was kneeling over him. He said simply, "Her Highness asked for you."

Kai rolled to his feet at once, hurrying toward the door to Signy's room.

Inside he found Signy standing in the middle of the room with her eyes closed, taking the kind of deep breaths that were a desperate effort to be calm and verged on hyperventilation instead. She was wearing only a bra and panties, and her face had been carefully made up, covering her natural loveliness with an almost identical mask.

His lion roared, but Kai knew that what threatened his mate now wouldn't need a solution as simple as fighting. He closed and locked the door and crossed the room to take her hands firmly in his.

"Signy. Listen to my breathing. Breathe with me."

He set her a slower pattern, not so frantically over-deep, and kept it up until her breathing had calmed with his. Her eyes opened, fringed with impossibly perfect black lashes and framed with faintly glittering eyeshadow, but they were still his Signy's eyes, the same as yesterday.

"You're going to be fine," he said firmly, putting all his faith in his mate into his voice. "What can I help with?"

Signy's pink mouth turned up in a smile. "Well, breathing, apparently."

Kai couldn't resist leaning in, brushing his lips as lightly as possible against hers. She licked her lips as he pulled away, and he licked his, tasting only the faintest waxy trace of her lipstick.

"Margrethe watched me do my face," Signy explained. "Then she said she had to go and wait for me at the airport, and she trusted me to get dressed and do my hair, but—"

"We'll get you dressed and do your hair," Kai said firmly. No one else would see his mate so naked, or so vulnerable.

He looked around and found a dress and stockings laid out on the bed, and steered Signy to sit again in the armchair. Her hands were still in his. She gripped tight as he guided her to sit, so he knelt before her, a guard to his princess.

"You can do this," he said softly, looking up at her. "You are your father's daughter, your grandfather's granddaughter. You were brave enough to come this far. You can do the rest."

Signy's mouth wobbled. "Can I do it without looking like a joke, though?"

Kai shook his head. "You'll look like what you are. A princess, more worried about doing her duty to her grandfather than spending a week picking the perfect clothes for the occasion."

Signy closed her eyes and took another slow breath. Kai kissed the back of each of her hands before he let go and stood, going to get her stockings from the bed. She watched him as he knelt again, and he said, "Would you rather do it yourself?"

She raised her hand to show him how it was shaking, and smiled as she shook her head. "I think you'd better. I'd snag them somehow."

Kai nodded and slipped a stocking over her foot. He smoothed it all the way up her thigh until the elastic at the top settled in place around the full curve. He glanced up at her and dared to press a kiss to the pale skin just above the top of her stocking.

Signy actually laughed a little, tapping one finger against

his lips. "Not now, Kai."

Kai gave a gusty sigh and moved on to the next stocking, but his lion was almost purring again with satisfaction. *He* had calmed his mate, even made her laugh. He would give her the confidence to show everyone what he had been first to see in her: that she was a worthy princess for Valtyra, brave and determined. Despite the way she had been left in the dark for so long about her family.

He stole another kiss at the top of the next stocking, just to see her smile again, but sat back before she could admonish him. "Dress next, or hair?"

Her hair was already drawn up away from her face, clipped in a simple knot, but he supposed it would require something fancier. As much as he loved the look of her dark hair tumbling down wildly over her shoulders, it wouldn't be a very proper style—nor practical, as windy as the airport was likely to be.

She gave a long look at the dress, then said decisively, "Hair. Simple but neat, Margrethe said. Sleek. There's a brush, and pins..."

Kai stood up and found them as well as a mirror, which he handed to Signy before he went around to perch on the back of her chair. He carefully unclipped her hair, combing through it with his fingers before he attempted the brush.

Signy tilted her head back, trusting herself to his hands, baring her throat. Her eyes were closed as she said, "I don't supposed you'd like to tell me a reassuring story about how you have a whole pack of younger sisters and used to do their hair all the time?"

He thought of Laila and winced. He wasn't going to bring up *that* story about his family with her, not when he was trying to reassure her.

"No, sorry," he said, carefully not explaining whether he had a younger sister or not. "But I used to watch my mother fixing her hair sometimes, when she was getting ready."

He let himself remember the motions of his mother's hands as he picked up the brush and drew it gently through the tumbling silk of Signy's hair, smoothing it back carefully from her forehead.

Concentrating on getting it just right, he added absently, "I have had some practice at grooming horses, though."

Signy laughed right out loud at that, and Kai couldn't keep a straight face either, though he managed to say, "How different can it be, really? Should I braid in some ribbons?"

Signy raised the mirror to look at what he was doing, and Kai winked at her reflection before twisting her hair into a smooth knot at the nape of her neck. "There, how's that?"

Kai made a few adjustments until all trace of hesitation vanished from Signy's expression, then pinned her hair in place. There was probably some clever way women knew to do it with half as many, but at least he was sure it wouldn't fall down by the time he was done.

He had hardly been aware of the plane around them as he worked on Signy's hair, but before he could go and fetch her dress, the pilot announced that they were landing. Signy's face turned serious again, and Kai sat down in the chair beside hers and took her hand between both of his.

Through the final descent and landing, he pressed kisses to each of her knuckles, each joint of each finger. Her eyes opened and fixed on him. Tension gave way again to warmth and something he felt sure had to be love, as warm and certain as his own. His mate, looking at him looking back at her.

When the plane came to a halt he stood, tugging Signy up with him. "Much as I hate to do it," he murmured. "We have to finish getting you dressed."

Signy turned her grip on his hand, raising his large, tan knuckles to the pink softness of her lips. She pressed a tiny kiss there, and then turned away to finish getting ready.

Kai felt his lion's satisfaction, and the anticipation of the battle yet to come. He'd done everything he could to prepare her for this moment. He could only hope he'd done enough, and that he would be able to protect her from everything she couldn't face alone.

5

SIGNY

Signy stepped out of her private room to face Tristan and the crew of the jet. Kai had slipped out to hurry into his formal Royal Guard uniform, so Signy was alone for the moment. She watched the faces of these Valtyrans for a more unbiased reaction than she would get from her mate.

She had slipped on a few pieces of jewelry that Margrethe had selected for her after Kai finished buttoning up her dress. The weight of gold and rubies at her wrist and around her throat, tugging on her ears, felt like anchors.

Or like armor. This wasn't just a fantasy of becoming a princess now; this was really happening. And just like every first day at every new school—not to mention every camp, commune, and festival—her mother had ever moved her to, Signy would get through this with her chin up.

She was still a little surprised when Tristan and the flight crew all swept into deep bows before her, without hesitation or so much as an amused, or shocked, look. She was truly their princess, now that they were in Valtyra.

She held herself a little straighter, and made the little hand gesture that permitted them to rise. Tristan, nearest to her, saw it first and straightened up most quickly, touching his hand to his heart in an additional small salute before he stepped back, clearing her path to the door.

Before Signy could move, there was a knocking from outside. The men of the flight crew all looked to her, while Tristan moved to get a view of who was knocking. From the corner of her eye she saw Kai step into the room and take up a position opposite Tristan.

She didn't dare look directly at Kai. She nodded to the flight crew instead. "Our welcoming committee, I suppose?"

The pilot smiled slightly, waving at one of his men to unlatch the door and swing it inward.

A woman stepped through—not Margrethe, but with something of her bearing and style. She had an even more harried expression than Margrethe had ever worn while giving a long-distance cram session to an entirely unprepared princess.

"This is Lady Teresa, Your Highness." The pilot, senior man present, stepped up to make introductions. "She is the head of protocol for the Royal Household."

Signy could see that Lady Teresa expected to have to try to do what Margrethe had done in five hours in the course of five minutes. Her eyes scanned over Signy, searching for some flaw.

"Ah," Signy said. "You must be Lady Margrethe's successor? Or have there been more between you?"

Lady Teresa snapped into focus, meeting Signy's eyes, and Signy knew that she'd scored a point.

Lady Teresa nodded slightly. "Lady Annaliese also preceded me. I believe both of them await us outside."

Signy nodded. "I believe she covered most of what I'll need to know." She saw Lady Teresa's lips tighten, thought of how easy it often was to get on a customer or boss's bad side.

She might be the princess here, but she couldn't afford to make enemies unnecessarily. "But she didn't know exactly what things would look like on the ground. Will you advise me?"

Lady Teresa's expression softened slightly, and she nodded again, stepping closer. Signy gestured back, and at Lady Teresa's faint nod they retired into her private room together. Lady Teresa walked a quick circle around her, tugging briefly at the hem of her dress. She scrutinized Signy's hair and makeup—and while she insisted on touching up Signy's eyeliner, Signy was proud to note that she didn't find a single stray hair to neaten.

As she worked, Lady Teresa went over a few simple points of etiquette—titles, greetings—with Signy, and Signy recited them all correctly. When Lady Teresa named the members of the council present, Signy raised her eyebrows and said, "Not Auxbrebis af Sparvhok or Van Zuylen af Bjorn, then?"

Both of them, according to Kai and Tristan's hesitant summaries, were likely to oppose Otto, more purely loyal to the king. Even better, Auxbrebis af Sparvhok was a sparrowhawk shifter, a distant relative of her grandmother.

Lady Teresa gave her a long look. She didn't ask how Signy knew the names or their significance. "That is correct. They did not wish to pressure you unduly. But... I think those who did wish to attend will not find quite what they were expecting."

"They should have expected the granddaughter of the king," Signy said firmly. It should have sounded ridiculous, but it felt true in her mouth.

Lady Teresa actually smiled slightly. "They should have indeed."

She swept back out past Signy, calling instructions to the guards and flight crew. Kai and Tristan stepped out before Signy had to try too hard not to look at them. And then it was Signy's turn.

She just looked out for a moment, focusing on the bit

of blue sky she could see through the open door, steadying herself. This was it. Signy stepped out through the door with a smile on her face, and then was stopped short at the top of the red-carpeted stairs. There was a line of men waiting for her past the end of the stairs, but beyond them was an enormous crowd—hundreds of people, maybe even thousands.

For a second, as she stepped outside, they were eerily quiet, and then a roar went up. Maybe a literal roar from some of them, she realized, though she didn't see any obvious animal shapes among the crowd. She glanced up at the birds circling nearby in particularly deliberate back and forth motions, and waved to them, thinking of the story Kai had told of her grandmother.

Then she waved to the crowd as well, and the roar somehow got louder. People were waving Valtyran flags and banners with the Asepnas af Bjorn crest. There were signs where she could make out her own name and little else. After a moment the tide of sound settled into a chant: *Princess! Princess! Princess!*

Signy couldn't help laughing with delight, thinking of where she'd been just a day before.

She glanced down and caught sight of one of the waiting men shifting impatiently—Otto—*His Grace the First Minister*—she realized, recognizing his gray hair and lean look.

She looked out to the crowd and waved again, refusing to be rushed. But it wouldn't do to make obvious enemies, either, or to have the council talking about how she obviously only wanted the attention of the crowds. Signy lowered her hand to the railing and walked down the stairs, keeping her chin up and watching the council, matching names to faces as she neared them.

The black-haired one who bore a faint resemblance to Tristan, though his skin was fairer and his eyes darker, must be Lord Gylden af Bagha, of the tiger shifter clan. Beside him was the youngest member of the council, Lord

Jessen af Varg—another wolf shifter, very loyal to Otto. That left Lord Kaas af Leijona, his golden hair faded with age to ash blond.

Tristan had looked at Kai when they were talking about him, and Kai shrugged, then shook his head. Signy had remembered that Kai was forbidden to speak of his family or clan. If Kaas af Leijona was some kind of relative of his, or likely to be sympathetic to a fellow lion shifter, Kai wouldn't speak of it.

All four of them bowed deeply to Signy as she stepped down onto the ground. She was faintly aware of her guards flanking her as she stepped forward, and knew only that neither of them was Kai.

The crowd quieted, and Signy looked up to find that everyone in sight had dropped into a bow or curtsey. She looked up for the birds who had been flying overhead. They had all found perches nearby, and leaned forward with wings spread wide.

The silence was eerie, and Signy remembered that she was here for more than just people chanting her name. They needed their princess. They needed her to choose their next king—and to help the king they already had, whether or not they realized it.

While no one was looking, Signy touched her hand to her heart. Then, as the nearest council members began to lift their eyes, she dropped her hand and signaled them to rise.

Otto straightened so quickly it was nearly an insult, but the other council members were slower. The crowd only gradually straightened up, a wave of motion that passed from the nearest to the furthest.

Signy offered her hand to Otto, inclining her head just so. "Your Grace. Will you present these gentlemen of the council to me?"

Otto looked as if he wanted to say *I was just about to*, but he swallowed the words and did as Signy had asked. He presented each of the lords of the council in turn, telling her much less than she already knew about each of them. Still, it was correct for them to be introduced, and Signy accepted each one's individual bow over her hand, murmuring her practiced thanks.

With that necessary ritual complete, Signy turned to Otto and said firmly, "I would like to see His Majesty as soon as possible, to learn how he wishes me to prepare for my duties as his heir."

And to beg him to give me and Kai his blessing so that we don't need to keep dancing around you, and I won't have to do this alone, she didn't say.

Otto gave her a condescending look. "Perhaps our long days have fooled you, Princess Signy. It is still very early in the morning here in Valtyra. It would not be suitable to roust the king from his bed just because you have been so hasty in arriving. I did tell you to take your time—"

Signy cut in before he could pretend that it was her fault that he'd made a great public spectacle of her arriving at four in the morning. "Naturally I would not interrupt the king's rest. But at his earliest convenience, of course I will wish to see him."

"Of course, at His Majesty's convenience," Otto agreed, as if she had given up something important.

She had a sinking feeling that it wasn't going to be *convenient* for the king to see her for a while yet. But clearly the whole country knew of her arrival, and her grandfather would wish to see her. How long could Otto really keep them apart?

Signy nodded graciously. "And in the meantime?"

Otto turned, gesturing theatrically to the crowds. "Well, if you are willing to accept such humble substitutes for His Majesty, there are a few other Valtyrans who are eager to make your acquaintance."

Signy could hear the sneer in his voice, and she could feel the gazes of the other members of the Council, judging her. But there was nothing to do but go forward. "Yes, of course, I'm happy to meet them."

Signy stepped forward without waiting for Otto to escort her, and her guards moved with her, still flanking her. Lady Teresa joined her as she walked toward the line of velvet cord that kept the crowd back. The cheering grew so loud she could barely think.

Lady Teresa guided her subtly until Signy spotted where they were going: Lady Margrethe stood with another elderly lady at the front of the crowd. Margrethe was holding flowers. She curtsied deeply to Signy, but Signy gestured her up almost at once, leaning in close to her to whisper, "Thank you."

"Thank *you*, my dear princess," Margrethe murmured back. Another cheer went up as Margrethe and Signy clasped hands with the bouquet between them. Then Signy had to be introduced to Lady Annaliese, and to Annaliese's young granddaughters, and so on and on and on down the line.

All the time, her guardsmen stayed just behind her, and all the time Signy was aware that neither of them was Kai.

~~*

Eventually Signy had greeted enough people. The sun was high even though it wasn't yet six in the morning, and she was whisked away in a sleek black car, driven by two guards who weren't Kai and Tristan. Lady Teresa shooed off all the members of the council and rode with her, but this wasn't exactly a respite.

"Let us review the itinerary for the day," Lady Teresa said grimly. Signy sat up straight and paid attention.

They returned to the palace, where Lady Teresa supervised a change of clothes. She was measured in the process, so more clothes could be made and tailored. Signy remembered to ask the names of the women who assisted her, but forgot them all instantly. Her brain was already a daze of new names and faces. Surely she would have time to learn them?

She let them dress her and touch up her makeup, but when someone went to pull the pins from her hair, Signy didn't think before putting up a hand to stop them. "Not that. Don't change it."

She realized as soon as she spoke that she couldn't tell them why: because her mate had put all those pins in her hair. It was as if he was still touching her, still with her, as long as those pins stayed in place.

She wasn't sure where Kai was now. He and Tristan must have had to report to the captain of the guard, and after all there was a whole rotation of guardsmen available now. Kai couldn't simply follow her everywhere, and it wouldn't do for Signy to ask for him or show favoritism before she had a chance to speak to her grandfather and gain his blessing.

It was just one day, Signy promised herself. By the end of the day she would have to have a chance to meet the king and speak to him, and they could settle all of this. She could get through one day.

But she couldn't bear to have a stranger undo what Kai had done with her hair.

"Please," Signy repeated, meeting the woman's eyes in the mirror. They were nearly the same amber color as Kai's, though her hair was a pale flaxen blond with no hint of lion-gold. "Please, just leave it."

The woman touched her shoulder gently and nodded, then picked up a comb from the dressing table. "I'll just neaten it up, and perhaps we can stick in some pretty clips for color."

Signy nodded quickly, her throat going tight with gratitude at not having to explain. Signy closed her eyes, letting herself be completely still for a moment while the woman worked on her hair, combing and spraying and adding more pins and clips.

Finally she said, "There."

Signy opened her eyes and found a princess looking back. Her hair wasn't just smooth but shiny-sleek like

68

something in a magazine, and jeweled clips glittered at her temples and the nape of her neck.

"We'll do another color at dinner, and add flowers," the woman informed Signy. "You don't have to let your hair down all the way until the end of the day. All right?"

Signy nodded again, opening her mouth to ask the woman's name, and then Lady Teresa was back to whisk her off to breakfast, an intimate gathering of thirty or so people. All of them were beautifully dressed, immaculately presented, all of them smiled and bowed or curtseyed to her, and none of them were Kai.

After breakfast there was a tour of the palace conducted by Lady Teresa and trailed by a half dozen other ladies from breakfast. Signy had briefly thought that this might be a break of sorts, other than walking miles inside the palace in her impractical new shoes—heels she would never have tried to wear to work.

She soon realized, however, that she was being shown off as much as the palace was. Every few minutes they encountered someone who just happened to be walking through that part of the palace, and Lady Teresa conducted introductions.

Signy was getting really practiced at responding correctly to all of it, even if she still couldn't remember a single name she'd been told. Eventually there was a lunch, slightly less intimate than the breakfast, with forty or fifty entirely different people in attendance.

She hoped they were different, anyway, and that she hadn't just forgotten everyone from breakfast already, but she knew it was possible.

She didn't see Otto, or anyone from the council. When she got a moment alone with Lady Teresa and asked about seeing the king, all she got was a tightening of lips and a little headshake.

After lunch she was allowed to rest. She was afraid "the princess needs to rest" actually meant another private session of being drilled on faces, names, and political affiliations, but it turned out that she really was being given time for a nap. She was helped out of her dress, allowed to wash her face and take the jewels out of her hair, and crawled into an enormous soft-sheeted bed.

She only managed to miss Kai's presence beside her for a moment before she was asleep.

~~*

The afternoon was more of the same, though she wore a different dress and was paraded through different parts of the palace. There were gardens overlooking the sea, a library full of books and parchments, many too delicate to touch, galleries full of portraits.

She was stopped in her tracks by the sight of herself as a toddler holding her father's hand. The portrait was nearly life-sized, with her father in a glittering uniform and her mother standing beside him in a dress of pale gold that set off her fair skin and the blazing red of her hair. The toddler version of herself wore a white dress, her hair a cap of dark, baby-fine curls, and she looked up at her father with a smile full of baby teeth.

She had never been here before, and yet it seemed she had been here all along. A small label on the golden frame explained: *Family portrait on the occasion of Princess Signy's second birthday.*

Signy didn't dare look closely at either of her parents in the portrait—she couldn't run away to the woods here if she burst into tears, and Kai wasn't here to come after her. Still, she had to look. It was obvious that she was supposed to be admiring this portrait of her own family (but not Poppy, and not the dad she'd grown up with— they were both utterly erased).

"It is a bit of an adjustment," a man at her shoulder murmured.

Signy fixed her practiced smile in place and turned to face him, glancing around as she did for her guards. They

70

didn't stay as close to her inside the palace; they were at the edge of the room now. She focused on the man who had spoken to her—not much older than herself, with ash blond hair and a lean build. His eyes were a warm brown, and she thought that she would have considered him very handsome yesterday.

He smiled slightly and tilted his head toward the portrait. "I've seen that portrait since I wasn't much bigger than you are in it. Logically I knew that you were growing up at the same rate, but it was hard to imagine you as an adult. And now here you are."

Signy couldn't think of what she was supposed to say to that, and reached for her stock of polite questions. She didn't dare ask his name, because they'd probably already been introduced at least once. Instead she said, "You've visited the palace often? Since you were small?"

He nodded, his expression turning slightly sheepish. "Well. My uncle, of course. And I've been working in the royal administration since I got home from university in Denmark."

She didn't need to ask who his uncle was; she recognized his wolfish build suddenly. He didn't have Otto's predatory look or gray eyes, but she could see the connection.

He was a wolf, a relative of Otto's, well-connected, well-educated, and had worked in the Palace ever since college. He had kind eyes, a gentle smile.

He might as well have been gift-wrapped. A... a *suitor*, offered to her without seeming forced. If she had been told yesterday that she had to marry this quietly nice guy...

But today was a world away from yesterday, and the thought made her feel cornered and almost sick.

He must have seen something in her expression, because he looked concerned, leaning closer and putting a gentle hand under her elbow. Signy wanted to pull away from even that touch, but she had to say something.

She shook her head quickly, looking away, and grasped

at the one straw she had, the one thing she knew she had to do to stop this from happening.

"I'm sorry. It just struck me. Working in the Palace, visiting so often, you must have met my grandfather—I mean, His Majesty—so many times, and I still haven't been allowed to see him myself."

"Well," the wolf suitor murmured, "his health really isn't good these days. I'm sure he'll be ready to meet you soon."

Signy murmured something inconsequential and looked away.

There was another charming young man in the gardens, and another at dinner. She didn't even try to remember their names. It didn't matter. None of them was Kai. She only had to get through the day, and get to the king, and tell him she had already found her mate, and then she wouldn't have to do this alone anymore.

She got through the entire endless day somehow, and found herself sitting at the vanity in her royal bedchamber. The same flaxen-blonde woman was attending her. This time, when she made to take the pins from her hair, Signy knotted her hands in her lap and didn't object.

"I'm sorry," Signy said, as the woman carefully removed one pin after another. "I'm afraid I've forgotten your name. And, um, your exact job."

The woman smiled at Signy in the mirror. "My name is Laila. I work for the royal household—we haven't had a chance to arrange for your personal staff yet, so I'm filling in a bit."

"Thank you," Signy said quietly. Then the name connected with something in her jumbled memories of her very long day. "Wait—Margrethe mentioned you, you're the one who got her to call me, aren't you?"

Laila smiled and nodded. "I was panicking a little, but I called Kai to warn him—"

Something strange happened to Signy's heart—it seemed to leap and fall all at once—at the sound of the one name she'd wanted to hear among the hundreds offered to her today.

She wanted nothing more than to be able to talk about Kai, but she didn't dare... and this woman spoke of him familiarly, and had his phone number.

It occurred to Signy for the first time that she *didn't* have Kai's phone number. She didn't have a single way to reach him. She didn't know his last name or anything about him, except how much he mattered to her.

"Oh," Signy said, aware in a way she hadn't been all day of how forced and artificial her voice sounded. "You know Kai?"

Laila stopped short, looking into Signy's eyes in the mirror, and then she dropped her gaze to Signy's hair, easing away the pins stuck in it. "Yes. He's... Royal Guards are required to renounce their families and clans when they begin their service, you know that?"

Signy relaxed at once, noting again the faint hints of resemblance. "But if he hadn't, he could tell me how he knew you?"

Laila's lips twisted. "Yes, although it would still be rather awkward. My mother is my father's second wife, you see—they are mates, but when they met my father was already married. He had a son who never forgave him for marrying his mate as soon as his first wife divorced him."

"Oh," Signy said in a small voice, at a loss for a moment. She could see why Kai might have been almost relieved not to be allowed to discuss his family.

"I have a younger half-sister myself," Signy offered after a moment. She forced herself not to pry for secrets Kai should be allowed to tell her himself. "My mother remarried after my father—that is, Prince Alexander—died. My sister Poppy was born when I was four years old, and I..."

Signy's throat tightened at the thought of Poppy. Where was she now? If Signy invited her to Valtyra, would she come? Would this be an adventure grand enough for her?

Would her *mother* be willing to come to Valtyra?

"I miss her," Signy said, when she realized Laila was still silently watching her.

Laila squeezed her shoulder, then went on unpinning her hair.

Signy washed her own face when Laila was done brushing out her hair, and changed into soft pajamas without more help than being pointed toward them. When she came out of the bathroom Laila was still there. She was holding Signy's phone, which had vanished with the rest of her luggage and all her normal clothes at some point during the day's constant flurry of activity.

Laila offered the phone to Signy, pulling another from her pocket as she did. "You'll need a new SIM card to connect to the network here in Valtyra—I'll get that sorted out for you by morning. In the meantime you should be able to get your contact numbers from your phone, if you'd like to use mine to call anyone."

Signy took both phones from Laila and sat down on the vanity chair to look at them. Laila had already unlocked hers; Signy tapped the button for Contacts without thinking.

Kai was listed first.

She could ask him to come to her—she could hear his voice—with just a tap of her thumb. Signy glanced up at Laila, who had turned half away, giving her privacy.

But if Signy called Kai, if she even texted him, Laila would know, and she showed no sign of knowing what Signy and Kai were to each other yet. If Kai had trusted Laila to help them make contact with each other, Laila would already know their secret, and she showed no sign of it.

Signy glanced at her own phone, but she didn't see any point in trying to contact Poppy or her parents. Not yet.

There was really only one person she needed to talk to, and as many times as she'd said it over the course of this endless day, she hadn't really *tried* yet, had she?

Signy set down the phones and stood up, looking around. Laila turned, focusing on her.

"I need a dressing gown, something I'll be decent in," Signy said.

Laila didn't question her, just nodded and hurried over to a wardrobe. She came back with a heavily embroidered dressing gown, all red and gold. It was nothing like the silk one she'd been wearing the night before; this one was stiff and quilted and nearly as heavy as an overcoat. Laila helped Signy into it and did up the hidden buttons that assured the dressing gown wouldn't flap open before she tied the sash.

"Thank you," Signy said. "Thank you for everything, today. You may go now—don't forget your phone."

Laila blinked at her, then nodded and dipped a little curtsey. "It's my pleasure, Your Highness."

Signy forced herself not to wince as she realized that she'd overdone the princessing a little. She hadn't meant to push Laila away quite so sharply, only to avoid dragging her into what Signy had to do next. But once she and Kai were together, and no longer had to keep their relationship secret, Signy would be able to explain it to Laila, and apologize for being so high-handed.

But before she could get to that, Signy had to speak to the king. To *her grandfather*, who had summoned her here.

She waited a moment after Laila had slipped out through the heavy door of the princess's bedchamber, listening until she heard the faint sound of the outer door of her suite closing. She counted to a hundred after that, taking slow breaths to calm herself.

Then she stood up and walked out the same way Laila had gone, out of her bedroom and to the outer door. When she opened it, the two uniformed guards there stiffened to attention, and Signy's heart sank a little. She hadn't really thought that Kai, or even Tristan, would be on duty there, but she had hoped, a little.

"Gentlemen," Signy said. "I'd like a word with you. Please come inside."

The two guards looked at each other. The older one had pale skin and jet-black hair, and his eyes were a muddle of amber and green. The younger looked barely older than Poppy or Laila. He had flame-red hair and a stocky build, and wore a slightly panicked expression as he looked to his fellow guard for guidance.

It was the older one who spoke. "Your Highness, the guard captain—"

"No," Signy said simply. "I am your princess, and you are both sworn to the protection of the royal family, is that not correct? You are loyal to us alone—my grandfather and me. That's what Tristan and Kai told me."

Their expressions calmed a little when she mentioned other guards, and she wondered how many guardsmen (and guardswomen?) there were. Few enough that they all knew each other?

"We are sworn to protect the royal family, as you say," the older one agreed. "But we are not servants, to follow your every whim."

Signy crossed her arms and squared her shoulders. "I only wish to speak to you. Regarding the safety of the king."

Signy turned on her heel and walked back inside, and both guards followed a moment later. The younger one took up a post just inside the door, and the older one came further inside. He touched his hand to his heart as he bowed to her.

"My apologies, Your Highness. I did not know how much you knew. My name is Andrej, and this is Peter. What is your concern for the king?"

"I only know what my guards have told me, so far," Signy said. "Which is why it is imperative that I see the king—my grandfather—myself. Why am I being kept from him?"

Andrej's lips tightened unhappily, and he nodded. "The

king is not well. The Crown Prince—your uncle—was of the opinion that a regent should be appointed, or the king permitted to go into retirement, allowing a new king to be crowned while he still lived."

Signy felt a tingling in her lips and fingertips, and the light in the room seemed suddenly brighter. "My uncle... who died suddenly, a few weeks ago."

Andrej's eyes widened, and he quickly shook his head. "Oh, no, Your Highness! No, nothing like that. He had been ill a long time—there are not many sicknesses that affect shifters, but he caught one when he was a young man, and it left him more susceptible thereafter. He fought it to the end. He still held out hope of finding a mate and taking the throne, but it got the better of him. None of us quite believed he wouldn't just fight it off again, so it was sudden in that way, but not unexpected."

Signy nodded slowly. "And my grandfather's illness?"

Andrej sighed, shaking his head a little. "He's never been quite the same since he lost the Queen. Those who lose a true mate never are—some can't survive at all with a broken heart. But His Majesty held on for the sake of his kingdom. Still, it takes a toll."

None of that sounded anything like a *diagnosis* to Signy, who was used to elderly people coming to the pharmacy and rattling off their list of intersecting and conflicting ailments.

"I wish to see him for myself," Signy repeated.

"But what if—" Peter cut himself off when Andrej shot a stern look in his direction, but Signy turned toward the younger guard.

"What if?" she prompted.

Peter glanced past her to Andrej, but tilted his chin up determinedly. "Your Highness. It's only—some have suggested that the king is only holding on until he knows you're here. What if, seeing you—what if he—"

Some have suggested. Signy studied Peter thoughtfully, wondering who was suggesting things to him.

"As far as I understand it, the fact that I'm here doesn't answer the question of who will rule next." Signy glanced back and forth between the guardsmen, looking for any hint of reaction, but they gave no sign of knowing her secret. "It will be whoever I marry who becomes the next king. And that can't happen until the king has given his permission for me to marry. So he must know that just my being here isn't the last of the things the kingdom needs him to do."

Still, a little tendril of fear crept through her heart. What if this was the only time she ever met her grandfather, the only time she could ever speak to him? What if the shock of seeing her, or the relief, was too much for him?

But if he were that close to the brink, surely he would be in a hospital, and there would be *doctors* saying these things to her, not just the Royal Guard. And if he were that close to dying, then she couldn't waste any time.

"I am the Princess of Valtyra," Signy said, straightening her own spine and tilting her chin up. "And I demand to see my grandfather, the king. The guards assigned to *him* can decide if he may not be disturbed; your responsibility is to escort me where I wish to go."

There was a silent second where she thought they would laugh, or refuse, or point out that yesterday she'd been an American pharmacy technician, and it was a bit much to be standing on ceremony as Princess of Valtyra now.

But she kept standing tall, determined to get through this moment one way or another.

And then Andrej stepped away from her side, striding briskly toward the door, and Peter wheeled around to follow him. Andrej looked outside, then looked back to her and nodded. "This way, please, Your Highness. Quickly."

Signy picked up the long skirts of her dressing down and hurried after him, silent on bare feet. They slipped out into the wide night-quiet corridor of the palace. It was only a short trip, down and across a short stretch; Signy was surprised to think that she had been so close all this time, but the suite they stepped into was too dark and still.

"There is a quiet way from here," Andrej explained. "These rooms are often—"

He stopped, turning to look toward the inner door with a frown. Peter stepped in, taking a defensive stance, just as the inner door swung open, and Signy braced herself to come up with a suitably royal attitude about being caught wandering the palace in the middle of her first night there.

But she didn't need to explain a thing. The man who stepped through the door was Kai.

6

KAI

Kai froze for a moment at the sight of Signy flanked by two of his brother-guards. His lion roared within him at the sight—*he* was the only one who ought to be protecting his mate—but he kept his face expressionless.

Signy was also keeping still, struggling to control her surprise. He saw the flush of heat in her face when she saw him, and the sight of his mate's reaction soothed the worry of lion and man both.

Andrej stepped into the gap, striding toward Kai as he broke the silence. "Kai? You're not on duty yet."

Even if Andrej hadn't seen the duty roster, that would be obvious. Kai was in his own off-duty clothes, dark jeans and a black sweater, and in a place he had no particular business being.

Kai nodded cautiously toward Signy. "I knew that Your Highness would be worrying about His Majesty. I visited him and was on my way to tell you of his present condition, but I assume you're on your way to see for yourself. I should have known you wouldn't rest until you had seen him."

81

Signy picked up his cue smoothly. "You were correct, Kai, thank you. Will I be disturbing him if I visit now?"

Kai let her see him wince, and had to control a worse expression when he saw that it hurt her to think of the king's condition. It would be worse, though, to let her see him without some warning. Kai had been surprised himself, and he had been close enough to observe the king's decline over the past few years.

"He is awake..." Kai hesitated, wanting, in this night-quiet place, speaking of her grandfather, to call her *Signy* or, with more affection than appropriateness, *Princess*. "Your Highness. But he is easily confused. Even after we introduce him to you, he may not entirely understand or remember who you are."

Signy looked startled, and Peter put in quickly, loyally, "He's better during the day, only tired and weak. At night he often can't sleep, but he's tired, and he gets confused."

"The king doesn't normally have audiences or formal duties past the early evening, these days," Kai explained. "I gather that he spent much of today with his council, working out the details about your formal welcome and how to prepare you for your royal duties. So he does know that you're here, though I'm not sure when he will be properly scheduled to meet you."

Kai also didn't know what Signy's schedule was. Frustratingly, he was assigned to administrative duties in the captain's office for the next couple of days, no guard details at all.

But that wouldn't matter if Signy could secure the king's permission.

If she persuaded the king to say the words tonight, when he was weak and confused... Kai felt a little sick at the thought, no matter how desperately he wanted to be allowed to be close to Signy, to openly claim her as his mate. The king was in no position to understand, or to give his true approval to their match.

No matter how sure Kai was that they deserved it, he

didn't like the thought of stealing that from the king he had sworn to serve and protect.

Still, the sooner the king had an heir in place the better off everyone would be, and that meant Signy had to marry *someone.* Kai couldn't endure the thought of her pressed to marry anyone else, and he knew the thought of it could only be worse for her.

"I'll just say hello and good night, then," Signy said firmly, straightening her shoulders and putting her chin up again.

She looked every inch a princess, wearing her embroidered robe like a ball gown. Kai bowed to her, quashing the conflicting urges to take her in his arms and lay her down on the nearest bed to find out what was under that robe.

He turned on his heel and pushed the door to the inner room wide again, leading the way. Neither Andrej nor Peter raised any objection, and neither of them seemed obviously suspicious. Andrej would warn him if he were giving himself away, Kai was nearly sure. Peter, he didn't know so well, since the young guard had been on the Crown Prince's detail.

Kai didn't look back or show hesitation, going directly to the hidden door that led to the secret passage to the royal apartments. Like every member of the Royal Guard, he knew the locations of all the secret ways through the palace as a matter of security. They all used them for personal convenience as well—though this particular passageway was really only a convenient path from the king's chambers to the wing that housed royal guests and distant relations.

Signy ought to have been housed in rooms nearer to the king's, but Kai supposed they had had to use the rooms that could be most quickly prepared for her arrival. Well, that could be fixed later.

The passageway was narrow, so there was no way to speak to Signy, let alone brush his hand against hers, on their way to the king's royal apartments. All too soon, Kai was tapping on the plain door, which swung back to reveal Magnus himself, the captain of the guard.

Kai smiled apologetically, though he didn't know whether it was his presence or Signy's that had brought Magnus here, or whether they had all stumbled across each other by sheer coincidence.

"Sir," Andrej said, more properly, as he stepped out of the passage. "Her Highness—"

"Here I am," Signy said, interrupting Andrej's attempt to speak for her. "Captain Magnus, isn't it? I wish to see the king; I ordered my guards to bring me, quickly and privately."

"Which explains what three of you are doing here," Magnus said, raising one dark eyebrow in Kai's direction.

"I meant to take news of the king to her Highness," Kai repeated, keeping his story simple and consistent. "But she was ahead of me, so I returned with her."

Magnus looked them over, then said briskly, "Her Highness does not require additional protection in the king's quarters. Andrej, Peter, back to Her Highness's rooms, before anyone questions why her door is unguarded."

Both of the guards retreated immediately, leaving Kai and Signy with Magnus.

"Your Highness," Magnus turned to Signy and adopted a stern tone. Signy stood her ground, and Kai clasped his hands behind his back to remind himself not to interfere between his captain and his princess. "Did your guards inform you that you cannot order them to do anything which endangers your safety, or the safety of the king?"

Signy was still for a moment, then raised her eyebrows. "I did not realize I might be in danger going from one part of the palace to another."

"You are not," Magnus agreed briskly. "But I do not want you to think that you will be able to order them to do anything you like, or that they may obey your orders at some cost to your safety. They have a sacred duty to your safety, and there is no honor in forcing them to choose between that and obedience to the Princess Royal."

Signy dropped her gaze for the first time, her cheeks flushing with shame. "I didn't mean to do that."

"You didn't, this time," Magnus said gently. "But it's a lesson that you ought to have learned as a child, so you had to hear it from someone in plain language."

Signy raised her gaze and nodded slowly, respectfully. "I thank you for it, Captain."

Magnus nodded back, then looked sharply between the two of them, and went on, "Now this part probably shouldn't to be said in plain language, but what's going on here?"

Signy looked at Kai, her eyes going wide, and this time Kai couldn't resist stepping in to rescue her. "She's my mate, sir, and I'm hers—we both recognized each other as soon as we met, back in America."

Signy darted to his side, obviously seeing no reason to keep her distance now that the cat was out of the bag. She exhaled when her hand slipped into Kai's, leaning subtly against him. Kai squeezed her hand in his and pressed his other hand to his thigh so he wouldn't wrap his arm around her.

Magnus sighed, his expression turning slightly pained before he frowned in thought. "Tristan knows, of course—and Otto doesn't know, but he suspects."

Kai gripped Signy's hand tighter just as her hand clutched his. "Suspects in general, because he's suspicious," Kai put in.

Magnus nodded. "Be that as it may—I have the orders I have, which are to keep both of you off the princess's guard detail and away from her. Ma'am, the council will tell you officially tomorrow, but they've got a half dozen eligible suitors lined up—"

"Oh," Signy said in a small voice, "I only spotted two or three today."

Kai forced himself not to tighten his grip on her hand—she was human, he could hurt her by holding on too hard if he wasn't careful—and contented himself with pressing his thigh closer against hers.

Signy glanced up at him, biting her lip as she flashed a little smile. "None of them were anything like you, oddly enough."

"By all means," Magnus said dryly. "Tell the first minister you prefer blonds. Only do it while I'm in the room, I'd like to see his face."

Kai managed, barely, not to run a hand self-consciously through his tawny hair. It wasn't quite a mane in this shape, but he did sometimes catch himself fluffing it out when he wanted to look taller.

Magnus went entirely serious again, shaking his head slightly. "Preparations are already underway for your wedding, Your Highness, to whomever you are persuaded to accept. It's set for ten days from now, and I don't think the Council means to reschedule just for one mostly-foreign young princess. Do you understand?"

Signy straightened her shoulders and looked past Magnus, to the door into the king's rooms. "I understand. I have ten days to convince the king that I know who I want to marry."

Magnus stepped aside, gesturing for them to go ahead. "Best not waste time, then."

Signy still didn't move from his side, so Kai gently tugged her with him as he stepped forward. She stayed close at his side all the way to the door, and Kai opened the door wrong-handed so he wouldn't have to let go of her, leading her inside.

The outer room was quiet, but there was a particular hush that fell inside the king's chambers. There were magics woven into the walls as well as the rich tapestries that hung on them—still important for warmth, despite the various modernizations that had been done here and there in the palace.

Mostly, though, it was the knowledge of being the presence of His Majesty, the King of Valtyra, first among shifters.

Signy went very still beside him at the sight of the king—white-haired but still tall and broad, a true great bear—standing by a window. He was turned half away from them, presenting the same profile that graced coins and stamps. His pajamas were covered by an embroidered robe not unlike Signy's, though the king's was more gold embroidery than silk, nearly as stiff as a coat of armor.

"Your Majesty," Kai said, pitching his voice respectfully low.

"Come and open this window," the king said, turning. "Who—Kai, isn't it? Open this window, she can't come back if—"

The king's eye fell on Signy, and he straightened up in some minute way, abruptly aware of having an audience. "Who have you brought to me?"

I have brought my mate, to beg your permission to leave your service and marry.

In the second of Kai's hesitation, Signy took a tiny step forward and sunk smoothly into the curtsey Kai had helped her to learn just that morning. He kept hold of her hand, steadying her as she rose to stand again.

"I am Prince Alexander's daughter," Signy said. "My name is Signy."

The king frowned. "But Signy is..." He looked toward the window again, where the queen in her hawk shape would never fly back home to him again, then returned a clearer gaze to Signy.

"I didn't think you would arrive so soon, my dear. Come here, let me see you. We need not stand on ceremony in private."

Signy hurried over to him, and the king set his hands on her shoulders, then touched her face.

"Signy, the little princess," he murmured. "Alexander's Signy. I've been waiting for you, my dear; you're needed."

Signy swallowed hard and nodded. "I understand, sir. I'll do my best for you."

"I know you will." The king turned, tugging Signy with him. "It's not so hard, really, only I can't seem to make the latch work. We must open the window again, you see, so the Queen can come home. She'll be so pleased to see you."

Kai took a step forward as Signy looked back at him with wide, worried eyes over the king's shoulder.

"Sir," Kai said. "Her Highness has had a very long day. She only came to wish you a good night."

There was no way they could ask him for anything, not like this.

Signy was nodding quickly, extricating herself from the king's grip.

"Highness...?" The king looked at Signy, puzzled. "No, Alex's American never liked that title, you mustn't call her that. You're taller than I thought, Mary."

Signy shook her head, and he could see her eyes filling with tears though she didn't let them fall. "That's my mother, sir. I'm Signy, Princess Signy. Your granddaughter."

"Signy," he murmured, turning toward the window again. "Just a child. Your mother should be here with you—guard, fetch Princess Signy's mother."

Kai opened his mouth to explain that Princess Mary had moved to America decades ago, but Signy went pale, looking horrified at the thought. Kai realized why an instant later. He could be sent to try to retrieve Signy's mother, just as he had been sent after Signy.

Only the errand would not be nearly so swift, and in the meantime Signy, his mate, would be here alone without him. If the king made the slightest mention of the idea to Otto, it could turn into a genuine royal order, and Kai would have no choice but to go where he was sent.

"No, please," Signy said hastily, drawing the king's attention. "Please, grandfather. You're right—she doesn't like all the princess business. She didn't want me to come, she was angry with me. I don't want her here at all, please don't send anyone to get her."

The king frowned. "A child should have family. A mother. The queen—" The king turned to the window again. "The queen will know."

"We'll ask her, tomorrow," Signy agreed. "But you should sleep. She wouldn't want you to stay up so late waiting, when your people need you tomorrow."

The king sighed and patted Signy's shoulder absently. "You're probably right. But the bed is so empty without her—well, you'll understand someday. When you find your mate, my dear."

Signy glanced at Kai and he knew that she felt the same empty ache he did at the thought that they must spend this night apart. And who knew how many more, before they could secure the king's permission, if he was so unable to give it at those hours when his council weren't constantly watching him.

"Maybe I'll find him soon," Signy said, her eyes still on Kai.

The king brightened. "Oh, yes. We'll find him for you. We'll make sure you meet every eligible young man. My councilors have thought of several you might like, and one of them is sure to do for you, and in the meantime you shall have a lovely party every night. You'll like that, won't you, my dear? I'm sure the queen won't mind if you borrow her jewels, and you shall have pretty new dresses."

Kai remembered Signy in her khaki pants and ugly green shirt, asking him if they could be together if he stayed in America with her, and he knew that she would give up everything the king promised to claim him now.

If only he weren't a guardsman. If only he could call upon his family's support, if he had any right to support from his father after spending years keeping his distance from the old man. But if he weren't a guard then he would never have met her, or only in the crush at some royal ball.

89

"Thank you, grandfather," Signy said, her voice small and choked. Kai saw her thinking of that same crush, all aimed at her, full of men determined to marry her and take the throne of Valtyra.

"Let me escort you back to your apartments, Your Highness," Kai put in, offering a hand. It was all he could do to rescue her from this situation, but thankfully it was enough.

The king waved Signy toward him, and she hurried over to set her hand on Kai's arm, which he folded in to draw her close to his side.

"Protect her with your life, guardsman," the king said sternly. "Kai, isn't it? You'll do all right. Go on, then, that will be all."

Kai wished he could pretend that that had been approval, or permission to do more than just return Signy safely to her rooms, but in truth he wasn't even sure the king knew who he was just now. He was the only Kai in the Royal Guard just now, but there had been two others in the years since he joined, and probably a dozen in the span of the king's reign.

The king turned away to the window again, and Kai drew Signy back out through the heavy carved door. The anteroom was empty. He took a moment to draw Signy close, hugging her to him to breathe in her scent and know that his mate was here and safe.

Signy freed her hand from his arm just to wrap both her arms around him, holding on just as firmly. "I won't," she whispered. "I won't choose anyone else. They can't make me, even if they do send you away. I'll come after you. I won't have anyone else."

"I know," he whispered back, nuzzling at her silky hair. "I know, Princess. You're mine and I'm yours. We'll make the king see. We'll make everyone see."

7

SIGNY

The next day, after a long night of tossing and turning in her empty bed without her mate, Signy was told she would be having a quieter day.

That quickly turned out to be a relative term. Her morning was filled with dress fittings, tutoring sessions on Valtyran history and government, more palace tours, and dance lessons.

"We'll need you passable on at least the waltz and one or two others in time for the ball," Teresa explained. "And that's only five days off."

"Oh," Signy said, remembering the fairy tale nightmare the king's words had summoned the night before. "I was afraid there would be one every night!"

"Well, there will be *some* dancing at the parties between now and then," Teresa said absently. "But those will be smaller, semi-private. You needn't dance, though it would be good to get the extra practice. At the ball all eyes will be on you when you take the floor for the first time with... well. With whoever you choose for your first dance."

The way Teresa said it made that much clear: Signy didn't have nine days to make her choice. She had five.

Whoever she danced first with at the ball would be taken by everyone to be her fiancé, who she would marry just a few days later.

She was briefly hopeful when her afternoon finally included an official meeting with the king. But Otto was there as well, and so was his nephew Stefan—Signy's wolf suitor from the portrait gallery—and a cousin of Stefan's who wasn't a wolf shifter but a bear. Tomasz was distantly related to the royal family, as well as to Otto. He had the big, broad build of a bear shifter, jet black hair and dark eyes.

He also had an astounding number of ways to try to touch her without seeming to do it on purpose. Even if Signy hadn't already had a mate waiting for her she would have hated him.

The fact that he kept trying to sneak those touches in with her grandfather, who was also *the king*, in the room, was even worse.

On the other hand, it wasn't like her grandfather was likely to notice even if Tomasz had thrown her over his shoulder and declared his intention to drag her off to bed right then. The king didn't say anything strange like he had the night before, but that was because he barely said anything at all.

He seemed dazed, his words slurred. He mostly responded with nods or shakes of his head, the occasional frown or smile. He seemed twenty years older than the tall, sturdy man who had stood with Signy the night before.

And when the clock struck three, Otto said, "Ah, your majesty, time for more of your medicine."

He took a small bottle from the tea tray and poured its contents into her grandfather's tea.

Signy frowned. "What is that?"

Otto gave her a stern look, and Stefan looked shocked; even Tomasz stopped trying to slide his hand over to her thigh to look at her like *she* had done something terribly rude.

"It's *medicine*," Otto said sternly, and held the teacup for the king to drink, which he did.

It was obvious that Signy wasn't going to get anywhere asking *what* medicine it was, never mind what condition the medicine was treating, or who had prescribed it and whether they were checking for interactions with any other medicines the king was taking.

Signy spent the rest of the tea dodging Tomasz's wandering hands and figuring out who she *could* ask. If Otto was doing more than just filling the king's ear, there had to be a way to stop him.

~~*

Signy didn't see Laila again until she was getting ready for the evening party. Two women, Katja and Dagmar, were still stitching a couple of the altered seams of her dress when Laila came in.

She handed Signy a tiny box, and Signy opened it to find a black microchip. She stared at it blankly for a moment and then remembered: Laila had promised to get her a new SIM card for her phone so it would work in Valtyra. She would be able to text her mother and Poppy, and if she could get Kai's phone number...

Signy looked up at Laila with a smile, feeling better than she had all through the long day. "Thank you! Um, but I don't know how..."

"I'll do it," Laila said. "Where's your phone?"

Signy could only move her left hand to keep from disturbing Katja and Dagmar's sewing, but she pointed. Laila went and found her phone on the nightstand and got to work on it.

Signy looked down to see how Katja and Dagmar were coming along with her dress. It was nearly done when she heard something snap into place, and Laila said, "There, now you can—"

She was interrupted by the chime of a text message

arriving, stuttering as it repeated two or three times. Laila hastily turned the phone away from herself, being careful not to see, and brought the phone to Signy's left hand.

Signy quickly unlocked the phone to be greeted by two new messages from Poppy in the group text with their parents. *Sounds like a blast! xx* and *Now you have to get an Instagram!! Europe's got lots of stuff to take pics of, right?* That one trailed off into a half dozen emoji—mountains, waves, and a crown.

Poppy probably meant it as a list of things to take pictures of in Europe: nature and royalty.

Signy looked down at herself, being sewn into a glamorous party dress so that she could be courted by men who wanted to win a kingdom along with the princess's hand in marriage. She let out a shaky laugh and blinked rapidly, trying not to cry and ruin her makeup.

She backed out of the text conversation, only to see that she had another message from Poppy, this one sent only to her: *I'm sure things are great but if it goes bad, lmk!! I can get you a couch to sleep on anywhere and I'll totally come kick some eurojerk's ass if he's mean to you. So glad you're taking a leap!* And then a string of multicolored hearts ending in the round-petaled flower which Poppy had chosen as the closest emoji translation of her name.

Signy closed her eyes, swamped with a wave of longing for her sister. She could ask for her now. She could text back, *Hurry, come to Copenhagen, I'll send someone to meet you, I need you.*

But Poppy would have even less idea what to make of Valtyra than Signy did. She would tell Signy to run, to abandon this whole impossible place rather than consider letting anyone corner her into marrying some stranger.

If Signy protested that she had to stay and help her grandfather, Poppy would come up with a scheme to kidnap him. *You've got friends with the guards, right?*

Signy laughed again and opened her eyes to find Laila watching her with a concerned smile. Signy realized that

Katja and Dagmar were gone; she was holding her careful pose for no one now.

"Thanks," Signy said to Laila. "Sorry, I—my sister."

Laila nodded understanding, then said hesitantly, "I actually came to go over the evening with you. Lady Teresa is up to her eyeballs wrangling the guests, but I'm one of her assistants. I thought you wouldn't mind me being the one?"

"Yes," Signy said immediately. "I mean, thank you, yes, I'm happy to have you do that."

Laila smiled a little wider. "It's my pleasure, Your Highness."

Signy smiled back, relieved at being understood. Then she thought, *Now would be a good time, she's said she likes you.* Signy took a deep breath and said, "Can I just ask a question first? I think I was rude today, and I didn't intend to be, and I'd like to know what I said. But asking is awkward because... I think I have to be rude to ask about it at all."

Laila made a face, acknowledging the awkwardness, but said, "I understand, Highness. I won't take offense, and I'll explain what I can."

Signy had been thinking all day about how to ask, whether there was any way she could ask just part of it. But now, standing here with Laila, she couldn't think why she should hold any of it back. "I'm worried about the king."

Laila's expression became guarded, but she nodded. "He is getting on in years, and since the queen—"

Signy shook her head quickly, pushing away the mental image of the king standing at the window, looking for his mate to come back. "I'm worried about his health. About the medicines he takes."

Laila's eyes widened. "Oh. And you asked...?"

Signy nodded. "We had tea today. Otto was there, and Otto's nephew Stefan, and another one named Tomasz, suitors—"

Laila covered her mouth with one hand, and Signy stopped there.

"So... pretty bad, then," Signy said, prompting Laila.

Laila dropped her hand and nodded, her eyes wide. "I can't think how to even—the king is not a figurehead, you understand? It's not like in human countries, where the king is just a symbol."

Signy nodded. She had understood that right away, from the way Kai spoke about it. It made a real difference to Valtyra, who sat on the throne. That was why she had to make the right choice.

"And the king *must* be a shifter," Laila went on. "Because, even if it hasn't actually happened in a hundred years, the king must be able to defeat any who would challenge his throne in single combat."

It was Signy's turn to stare, dumbfounded. "But he—he couldn't possibly—"

Laila nodded quickly, waving Signy's words away with a sharp gesture. "He could have, in his prime. And even now, who knows what his bear could do if a challenge arose? Those of us who work closest to the king, who see the most of his condition—we might say quietly, among ourselves, how he hasn't been the same since he lost the queen, that he's getting on in years. But to bring up his—his ailments—publicly, or in front of those who might challenge him—it is to suggest that he should no longer be king."

But he shouldn't, Signy thought rebelliously. *He's old, he needs care, he should be allowed to retire, he should be in a hospital.*

She couldn't say that; she couldn't even suggest it, even to Laila. That was clear. Thinking back, Kai had been very careful how he said things, and so had the other guards.

"But when I choose someone, a shifter, to be my husband, to become the king's heir, what then?"

Laila shrugged, spreading her hands. "There's no telling, Highness. It might be the Council names the new prince as regent for the king, or the king may even be allowed to step down from the throne, just as if there had been a challenge. Then the new king could set the conditions of his retirement, give him an estate to live on..."

"But when exactly is it okay to ask what's wrong with him?" Signy put in sharply. "When does he *see a doctor*?"

Laila gave her a pained look. "Shifters... mostly don't, Highness. They can heal quickly from nearly anything. The things they can't heal—either they die, or... or they are made weak. For shifters of a lower status there are healers, and nowadays there are even some who study human medicine and seek to apply it to shifters. But the *king*..."

"But he takes *medicines*," Signy insisted. "Who is prescribing them? Who is making sure he takes the right ones, and that they don't interfere with each other?"

Who can tell me whether Otto is drugging my grandfather, or poisoning him, or honestly trying to help?

Laila's helpless look made it obvious that there wasn't going to be a good answer to Signy's questions. And no matter how close Laila was to Kai, Signy didn't dare put all of this on her. She needed to talk to Kai. The Royal Guard had to be able to consider how to protect the king, even if no one else could speak of it.

She needed Kai at her side more than ever.

"Laila," she said, "could I borrow your phone for a moment?"

Laila frowned but nodded and handed it over, unlocked, along with Signy's.

Signy didn't let herself think, even though her fingers were trembling, as she copied Kai's contact information to her own phone. She carefully didn't look at the messages he and Laila had exchanged. This wasn't about checking up on him. She needed him. The king and Valtyra needed him.

And if she was aching for the sound of his voice, the touch of his hands, well. Maybe she could do something about that, too.

But first, she had to get through tonight's party.

"Sorry," Signy said, handing Laila's phone back and taking her own to tuck under her pillow. "You were going to tell me what I need to know for the party tonight?"

Laila smiled, obviously relieved to be back on track, and started reviewing the guest list.

~~*

Signy fell into bed that night, aching from her feet to her head from the long party and the intense concentration required every moment to make sure she wasn't making horrible mistakes.

Tomasz, with the wandering hands, and Stefan, kind and polite, had both been in attendance. So had Gregor, so quiet and reserved that she would have doubted whether he was being set up as a suitor except that Otto had introduced him to her—and that, quiet as he was, he wouldn't have paid such pointed attention to her if he hadn't had some purpose in mind.

Signy had had to dance with Stefan and with Gregor. She had managed to evade Tomasz all night, but who knew how long she could keep that up? Even polite and gentle hands touching her made her feel a little sick, knowing that they weren't Kai's, and that time was running out to make sure that she could choose Kai for herself.

She wanted to cry by the time the party was over, or to crawl under her covers and refuse to come out for anyone but the one person she wanted to see. But she let Katja extricate her from her dress, smiling and thanking her. She let Dagmar take her hair down and supervise her removing her makeup, and thanked her too, even though she missed Laila's quiet, understanding presence.

And then, when she was finally alone, grateful for the silence and aching for the absence of the one person she wanted, she was free to pull out her phone and touch her finger to Kai's name.

"Hello," he said, and her body flushed hot at just the sound of his voice and the promise of contact, before his recorded voice continued. "This is Kai. I can't answer my phone right now, please leave me a message. I'll get back to you as soon as I can."

The message repeated afterward in Valtyran, which she half understood, and she wondered if he had changed the message just recently, so that the English version would come first, so that she would hear him say *hello* just for her.

She hung up without leaving a message, feeling too near to tears to speak without crying. She stared at her phone for a moment, wondering what to do. She had no idea how long it might take for him to be able to check his phone; he might be on duty anywhere.

Someone would have told her if he had been sent out of the country again, wouldn't they?

No, Kai would have found a way to tell her.

Signy squeezed her eyes shut and made herself tap out a quick text instead of continuing to fret over the possibilities.

This is S. Call me when you can.

She wanted to add *I love you*, or even just a string of hearts, but she didn't dare. There was no knowing who might catch a glimpse of his screen. Whether he had recorded his message with her in mind or not, he wouldn't be expecting her to call.

She hit send, pushed her phone under her pillow again, and lay down for another night of attempting to sleep in her too-big empty bed without her mate.

~~*

Signy woke up at the sound of something tapping on her window. She didn't know where she was for a moment, and then the tapping repeated and she sat up sharply.

She was in her enormous room in the palace in Valtyra.

Across from her bed, heavy curtains covered diamond-paned windows she had only had a couple of chances to look out through. She knew that there was nothing outside her window but a steep drop and a picturesque view, facing inland over the black roofs of the capital city, and beyond that, the green mountains that occupied the center of the island.

If a bat was tapping at her window, it might also be a person. But maybe it wasn't a bat at all. Maybe...

Signy groped under the pillow for her phone, but she was already slithering out of her huge bed. She hurried over to the curtains and tugged them open. It was dark outside, one of the few hours of real night, and for a moment she didn't see anything at all.

Then a familiar hand reached up and splayed wide against the window, and Signy realized that Kai was clinging to the stone wall just below. She hurriedly undid the latches and swung the windows open. Kai grabbed the sill and hauled himself through.

Signy backed up a couple of steps to give him room, so she had a half second to see the dark gray clothes he wore before he closed the distance between them. Then his arms were around her, crushing her tight against him. He kissed her fiercely, stealing her breath.

Signy raised her arms to wrap around his shoulders, moaning into his kiss and holding on with all her strength. She had needed this, needed him, so desperately that the longing for him had become like white noise, filtered out like the sound of the sea. But now that he was here, all her hunger for her mate awakened again. She couldn't let go of him, couldn't even break the kiss to breathe.

Her hands moved down his body, feeling the hard strength of him through his clothes, and he groaned into her mouth. "We should—"

"I know," Signy breathed back. She had so much to ask, to tell, but she couldn't stand to stop touching him yet. Her fingers found his belt, and she slid her hand lower, finding the bulge of his hardness. "But couldn't we—first—"

Kai caught her mouth in another kiss instead of replying in words. His hands moved down to her hips, hot through the thin cloth of the nightgown she wore. He pulled her up against him, and she wrapped her legs around him when her feet left the ground, pushing the hem of her nightgown up to bare her thighs. For a moment Kai just held her there, his kiss hot and fierce as she clung to him.

When he did move he turned back toward the windows, pressing Signy's back to the cool glass and allowing her to perch, barely, on the narrow sill. She let her legs fall open, giving Kai room to slip one hand between her thighs as he kept kissing her. She moaned when his fingertips traced over the sensitive folds of her, already wet with her eagerness for him.

"Princess," he whispered. "Signy—"

"Kai, please, I need you, I need you." Signy reached for him again, finding the hardness of him and stroking him through his jeans.

He nearly growled, and the fierce power in that sound made Signy moan. She felt hotter and wetter than ever knowing that she was driving her mate wild with just a touch, the same as he did for her. Kai kissed her again, mercilessly claiming her, and she was only faintly aware of the sounds of him undoing his belt and fly at the same time.

He touched her again, pushing fingers into her slick folds, driving deep into her, but not deep enough. She pulled away from his kiss to gasp, "Please, Kai—"

And then his fingers were gone and she felt him entering her, thick and hot, and this time there was nothing between them. This time they wouldn't hold back from this, or pretend that they might be willing to be parted. As he pushed slowly inside her, Signy could feel every inch of him and knew that there was no going back, however much she might have to pretend. She belonged to Kai, and he to her, and that knowledge, as much as the feeling of him inside her, made her shudder with bliss.

She tightened her legs around him again, drawing him in and trying to keep him close as he moved inside her. He rocked his hips, moving inside her in delicious little thrusts that hit right where she needed him, and his hands skimmed up from her hips, under the nightgown she was still wearing. He cupped her breasts, rousing a pleasure that echoed the motion of him inside her. When his thumbs rubbed over her nipples she tipped her head back against the window, gasping, her whole body tightening around his.

He kissed her throat and moved harder inside her, wringing more and more pleasure from her until she couldn't take it. She cried out as her climax washed over her, quickly muffled by his mouth over hers. She felt his body go taut as he came, his hardness jerking inside her, filling her.

They would be married so soon, she thought giddily. What did it matter if they got started a little early on their first prince or princess?

A second later she heard a knock on her door, and Kai, who had started to relax against her, tensed in a whole new way.

"Yes?" Signy called out quickly.

"Your Highness?" It was Andrej, the guard who stood at her door at night. Had she been that loud, before Kai quieted her? Or were shifter senses that sharp? "Is everything all right?"

Kai shook against her—inside her, where they were still joined. Signy realized he was trying not to laugh.

"I'm fine," she called back. "Just... just a dream."

There was a little pause, but then Andrej called back, "I see. Sleep well, Highness."

Signy squeezed her eyes shut as she called back, "I will!"

She waited a moment, straining for the sound of the outer door closing as he went back out to the corridor. She didn't hear it, but she guessed Kai did when he lifted his head from her shoulder and let out a faint, breathy laugh.

Signy shoved against his shoulder, trying not to laugh herself. "You should have warned me they would hear!"

"You didn't give me much chance to," Kai pointed out, but he kissed her again as he stepped back from the windows. She thought he would set her on her feet, but he carried her across the room instead, all the way to her bathroom.

It was even darker there than in her bedroom, without the open curtains or the small nightlight that kept the room from being pitch black when the curtains were closed. Signy clung to Kai in the darkness, even when he set her on her feet.

He murmured, "Princess, you mustn't have the scent of me in your bed, or on your body, when your ladies come to wake you in the morning."

Signy shook her head, not letting go yet. "I have to talk to you. I meant to..."

Kai kissed the top of her head and closed his arms around her, still holding her close. "Yes."

"The king," Signy added, moving instinctively to tug her nightgown down as she raised the topic of her grandfather.

Kai shifted too, rearranging his clothes, but then he was holding her again in the dark. Signy leaned into his body, reveling in his warmth and strength, his familiar smell; quite aside from the pleasure of having him, it was so good to be close to him.

"Tell me about the king, Princess." He accompanied the words with a kiss at her temple.

Signy sighed and forced herself to think, remembering what she'd seen, what Laila had said. She found herself standing up straighter, and Kai's arms slipped down, giving her a little breathing room without letting go.

103

"He's sick, isn't he? But no one will say, because no one can admit that he's weak, that he couldn't defend himself if someone challenged him for the throne."

She felt Kai go rigid.

Signy sighed. "I'm human, and his granddaughter, and you're sworn to protect him. Neither of us could ever, ever challenge him. That's the only reason I'm saying this to you."

Kai exhaled, rubbing up and down her back with one hand and bending his head to rest his forehead against hers. "It's still... hard to think of. The Royal Guard exists mainly to protect the queen and the children of the royal family. And to be the king's right hand if it comes to more than a challenge, if there is open war."

Signy took a breath of her own. It was obvious that, even if it hadn't happened in a long time, it was a very real possibility to Kai. "That's what could happen if there were no heir? If the king died, and no one had been chosen—people would challenge each other? Fight it out?"

Kai nodded. "And it's only supposed to be one against one, but... things used to happen; people have families, pressures can be applied."

Signy closed her eyes, thinking of the men she'd met—quiet Gregor, courteous Stefan, pushy Tomasz, and how many others who would think they were better for the job? She imagined them all fighting each other, sending their families against each other. The pretty, spacious palace could transform into a battleground at any moment.

Signy looked down at her hands, remembering Otto pouring from that little vial. Otto was the one they were worried about, really, wasn't he?

"Does it ever happen that a member of the council challenges the king?"

She felt Kai flinch, and his voice was even more cautious when he answered her. "Yes. The heir is normally on the council, for one thing, but, yes, it does happen. Openly, publicly. A fair fight."

"But he's not fighting fair," Signy said quietly. "Is he?"

"That would be a very serious accusation, if anyone were to make it," Kai said, equally quietly, almost whispering. "There would have to be very clear proof for the Royal Guard to act openly against the First Minister. And we can find no proof. He is careful, he works in the background, doing nothing obvious that we can fight against."

"The medicine he gives the king?"

Kai shook his head. "A normal calming draught. There has never been any sign of poisoning or overdose."

"I saw other bottles in his room the other night. Is the calming draught Otto gives him the only medicine he takes? Has anyone diagnosed him with any particular illness?"

"Magnus had a physician look at him, and a traditional healer. They each had their own opinions, so there are a few things he takes, some pills, some potions."

Signy winced. "Kai—before all this, I worked in a pharmacy. Dispensing medications, you understand?"

Kai frowned, but nodded. "Humans are—"

Signy shook her head quickly. "I wouldn't presume to prescribe anything for him, I wasn't even a full pharmacist, just a tech. But I do know that two medicines that are both beneficial by themselves can be dangerous, even deadly, in combination."

Kai straightened up; the little light there was in the room reflected off his eyes as they widened.

"Interactions can cause all kinds of weird results," Signy pressed on. "And we don't even know all the possible interactions and combinations. Add in different body chemistry, different illnesses—it wouldn't even have to be malicious, Kai. That many different medicines could be making the king worse purely by accident. And if more than one person prescribed things without consulting each other, he may be getting too much medicine for whatever is really wrong, which could be causing all kinds of side effects."

"Otto would have been one of the first to notice anything like that," Kai murmured, frowning. "Easy enough then to cover everything else with a calming draught..."

"The king needs to see a doctor," Signy pressed. "Or the doctor and healer together, with someone who knows the properties of all the medicines he's taking. If it has to be secret, if only Magnus can arrange it—please, Kai, for my grandfather's sake, someone has to find out what's happening. And if it's *not* an accident..."

Kai nodded decisively. "I must go then. No time to lose."

Signy sighed and nodded back.

"I'd rather stay," he murmured, leaning down to kiss her softly. Just that was enough to send a thrill of heat through her whole body, despite the faint soreness between her legs. If there were more time, if he could only stay all night... "If I could—if it weren't so dire—"

"I know," Signy whispered. "But if we can get the king well enough to give his permission—or prove that Otto must be removed—then we can be together always, right?"

"Always," Kai promised, giving her one more lingering kiss. "But first, the king. I'll tell Magnus what you told me. We'll find a way, I promise you."

"I trust you," Signy assured him. "But we only have a few days. The ball..."

Kai nodded, already going back toward the window. "I'll be there, Princess, I swear to you. Don't dance with anyone else before me."

8

KAI

Kai barely saw the inside of the palace for the next two days, let alone catching sight of Signy. Magnus kept Kai and Tristan out of Otto's sight by sending them on endless errands no one else could be trusted with. Kai even flew to London to speak to a handful of Valtyrans studying medicine at a university there. He returned the next morning to report what he had been told, then later in the day escorted two doctors from a ship to the palace in an anonymous van.

Signy didn't send him any more texts, but Laila texted him from time to time. On the second night she sent a photo of Signy in her formal finery. Kai's heart thumped painfully with desire and his lion roared at the continued separation from his mate.

Things were progressing, though. The men Kai had brought in took samples of all the various concoctions the king was dosed with and mixed secret replacements for them, ones that would appear the same to Otto and whatever servants he had suborned, without being dangerous to the king.

His condition did not improve instantly, but Magnus seemed confident that he would mend. It was only a question of whether there was time, and whether, even without the effects of the medicines, Otto would still hold his ear.

The day of the ball for the Princess Royal's formal debut arrived, and Kai was aware of the buzz of gossip around the palace. Stefan Sparre af Varg, a nephew of Otto's, was thought to be the princess's favorite, but she had made no clear choice yet. Kai controlled his own reactions, letting nothing slip, until Magnus took him aside in the early afternoon.

"You intend to be at the ball tonight?" Magnus said quietly.

Kai nodded. Every member of the guard would be attending, in their most resplendent uniforms, to form an honor guard for the Princess Royal as she was presented formally for the first time.

Magnus sighed. "If I order you away, or forbid you to approach the princess..."

Kai's lion roared within him; he almost thought, from his tiny wince, that Magnus heard it. "Sir. I made a promise to my mate."

"You are sworn to the Royal Guard," Magnus said sharply. "Until you are released with the permission of the king, you have no mate, no family. Nothing but your duty and your honor."

Kai gritted his teeth, but only repeated, "Sir."

Magnus sighed, shaking his head slightly. "I had hoped that there would be some chance today. The king is doing better with my efforts to limit his medications, I think, but Otto has him in council all day. The calming draughts may take a long time to wear off. If you wish to speak to the king, your best chance may be late in the evening."

Signy's first dance would be the sign of her choice, and it would be early evening, the sun still high, when the ball opened. "*Sir.*"

"If you wish to be a thief, or an oathbreaker, do what you must," Magnus said sternly. "If you wish to speak to the king, listen to what I say, and *wait.*"

Kai nodded grimly. "Understood, sir."

~~*

Kai was placed among those guards who took position around the royal thrones in the ballroom, marking out the royal territory in the great shining room while the most eager guests arrived early. The light outside was still bright. The sun would not set until hours into the ball, on this summer evening in the far north.

When dark falls, Kai told himself. *When it is dark, I will speak to the king.*

The room slowly filled with people. The men mostly wore brightly-colored uniforms representing their family and clan affiliations, while women were gowned in every dazzling shade of the rainbow. All wore their human shapes and none carried weapons. To shift or draw steel in the presence of the king on such an occasion would be seen as the opening of an attack.

A large crowd had gathered by the time the doors at the side of the room, reserved for the use of the royal family, were flung open. The heralds pounded their staffs on the shining parquet floor, and the red uniforms of the guards around the king and princess were visible through the doorway.

Kai and the men around him snapped into motion, a long-practiced bit of ceremony. They formed up into ranks, marching forward until the rearmost two were on the lowest step of the dais. The rest marched through the crush of the ballroom, clearing a path, with pairs of guards taking up station every five paces—sixteen feet apart exactly, so that they would be evenly spaced from the dais to the doors. Kai was in the first pair to stop, sixteen feet from the thrones.

It meant Signy would walk three-quarters of the distance to the dais before she passed him. For forty-eight feet, she would be able to look at him, and he at her, without either of them doing anything so obvious as to turn their head.

The foremost pair of throne guards met the escort guard at the doors and executed a crisp turn, reversing to take the lead in the formation as the king and princess entered the room. All the onlookers had gone quiet.

It was the first time since the Crown Prince's funeral that the king had been seen so closely by so many; mourning had been put aside for the princess's welcome. Before that, it had been more than three years since the king had held a ball. Most of those gathered were as curious to see the king in these conditions as they were to meet the princess.

The king stepped into sight, wearing a simple black suit that made him instantly visible among the bright red and gold of the guards. If his eyes still seemed a little dim, his posture was straight and he had a practiced, familiar smile on his face that made even Kai feel reassured for a moment. The king wore a simple gold circlet on his thick white hair, and the jeweled chain of a royal order draped over his shoulder, the central plaque resting over his heart.

The crowd roared approval, and the king paused just past the doorway to wave, then gestured for quiet.

As one, every voice in the room fell silent, watching even more intently as the king turned and offered his hand, and Signy stepped into view.

Kai's heart soared at the sight of her, and his lion roared louder than the hundreds of people gathered around.

Signy was resplendent in a gown of white under elaborate gold and red embroidery, so thick and intricate that the background color was barely visible, except by contrast with the darkness of the king's clothes. Her curves were all highlighted by the gown, her bust framed by the neckline to show off the creamy bounty decorated by one of the finest gold and ruby necklaces from the queen's collection.

She waved, and he caught sight of the jewels wrapped around her wrist, and then he finally dared to look at her face. She was smiling—an expression as practiced as the king's—and her dark hair was piled up in intricate twists with a tiara set on top.

For a moment Kai couldn't see anything but *Her Royal Highness, the Princess Royal.* Then she turned her head as the king began to lead her forward, and Signy's eyes met his.

His mate didn't let her step or her expression falter, but her eyes widened just enough to let him know that she felt what he felt at seeing her again after days apart. His heart thundered. It took all his years of training and discipline just to stand still as the king led her toward him. He watched a flush rise on her cheeks, even after she forced herself to look away from him.

Kai did not allow himself to smile, but his lion roared.

He fell in with the others after the king and princess had passed, joining the end of the honor guard ranks. The king climbed to his seat on the throne, handing Signy over to hers; he took his seat first, then waved her into hers, and Signy gave a sweet little curtsey before she sat.

The honor guard, in perfect unison, all dropped to one knee before their king and the princess. He knew that behind them all the guests at the ball were bowing and curtseying as well, honoring the royal guests of honor.

"Rise, rise!" The king's voice was nearly as strong as ever, and more welcome than it had ever been, because it gave Kai leave to look toward Signy again, just in time to catch her eyes sweeping away from him. She was being careful not to stare.

But they wouldn't have to be careful for much longer. Only hours, if she would just give him time...

Kai moved into place automatically, taking up his

assigned position at one side of the royal dais while half the guards spread out to take up ceremonial positions around the grand ballroom. He was on the king's side, not Signy's. He could only see her in his peripheral vision, but he could see the way any man would have to approach to request a dance.

It would be now, if it was going to happen. The king raised his hand, gesturing for the music to begin, and the crowd drew back, making room for the dancing. Kai saw a few men moving forward—Stefan Sparre af Varg off to his left, and two others he recognized.

Signy sat back pointedly in her royal seat and made a gracefully dismissive gesture. She was saying as clearly as if the herald had called it out, *I'm not dancing yet.*

A ripple of uncertainty and curiosity went through the crowd, but Lady Margrethe moved forward to begin dancing, escorted by one of her nephews. Others hastened to follow her sterling example. The dance floor filled without the princess choosing a partner, and Kai allowed himself to breathe a tiny sigh of relief.

Signy was waiting for him. He just had to find his chance.

9

SIGNY

Signy's first refusal to dance only got her to the end of the first piece of music, as Margrethe had warned her it would. Near the end of the dance, Signy turned to her grandfather, who was looking more and more alert. It gave her hope that she would be able to ask him for permission to choose her own partner by the end of the night—before the Council could whisk him away behind closed doors again, or Otto could find some new secret way to manipulate him.

For now the king still seemed a bit foggy and absent, and Signy said only, "You don't mind if I go and circulate a little, do you, Your Majesty?"

"Not at all, my dear, it is your party. Only, choose your first dance wisely." He frowned a little, then added hesitantly, "We should have spoken more about that before now, and now is not the time..."

"It's all right, Grandfather," Signy said quietly. "I know what I must do."

He nodded and reached out to pat her hand. "Go on,

then, my dear. Enjoy your party."

Signy smiled, and it even felt genuine, with the hope that she felt rising in her. If she and Kai could just find the right moment tonight, then this could all be settled soon. "I will."

There was no way for the Princess of Valtyra to be unobtrusive at the ball in her own honor, but Signy had had a lot of practice in the last few days at ignoring stares. She got down off the dais and turned to greet the first person she recognized—a distant cousin on her grandmother's side, Elisa Auxbrebis, who was standing nearby.

"It's been such a whirl," Signy confessed to Elisa, linking their arms together. "I fear I have forgotten more names than I've learned this week. Will you be my guide while I circulate?"

"Of course," Elisa agreed. Her look said she understood that Signy welcomed her help in avoiding dancing as much as anything else.

Signy gave a tiny smile and shrug back, and then she was able to walk with Elisa around the perimeter of the ballroom, having people helpfully pointed out to her. Signy kept an eye out for the suitors she already knew to expect; it didn't take long before Stefan approached.

Elisa released Signy's arm as Stefan bowed, but she stayed close. When Stefan straightened up, he looked into Signy's eyes a moment, then leaned in to say quietly in her ear, "We would not make such a bad match, Signy."

It was the proposal she had carefully evaded all week, distilled down to a single unromantic sentence. If she had truly wished to find a husband among the men offered to her, she might have agreed with him.

"I am honored by your attention," Signy returned quietly. "But my mind is made up."

Stefan drew back to give her another thoughtful look, this time frowning slightly. Signy was reminded that, as polite as he had been, he was Otto's nephew. Still, he gave her another slow nod, nearly a bow, and bowed as well to Elisa before he slipped away into the crowd.

"One down," Signy said under her breath, and then she took Elisa's arm again.

Six more dances went by while Signy moved around the room, making cheerful small talk and ignoring all hints that she ought to choose a partner and step out on the floor. Elisa stepped firmly on Tomasz' foot so Signy didn't have to ("He was like that when he was ten and taking dancing lessons, too," Elisa muttered darkly) and at some point she looked up to find Gregor watching her from the other side of a small circle of conversation.

He tilted his head, raising an eyebrow. Signy tightened her lips and gave a tiny shake of her head. Gregor nodded, touched his hand lightly to his heart, and turned away, walking off without a word.

If only everyone would make as little objection to letting Signy make up her own mind. After they'd made a complete circuit, Elisa led Signy out onto a balcony to catch her breath. Two of the red-uniformed guards— Peter, along with someone she didn't recognize—flanked the door she had come out through. Signy took their protection as a promise that she could have a few moments of quiet.

In truth, it wasn't entirely quiet out on the balcony. Directly below her feet was a part of the palace gardens, but she was high enough to see over the wall that bounded the gardens.

On the other side, a long way down from where Signy stood, was the sea, crashing loudly enough that she could barely hear the music from inside. The long twilight was streaking the still-bright sky in brilliant colors, and Signy stood and looked for the first stars, not thinking of anything at all.

She heard a little noise behind her and turned, jerking back when she realized that Otto was close enough to touch her. He said nothing, simply looking at her with his icy cold eyes.

It occurred uncomfortably to Signy that this was the first time she had been alone with him since he told her who she was. Only Kai and Tristan weren't just outside now, and Signy, all dressed up for the ball, was a long way from the driver's seat. She didn't think she could run far, either, not in these shoes.

Otto would only have to step a little closer and he could push her right over the railing.

She saw his gaze sharpen, as if he could tell what she was thinking. Could wolves smell fear, even when they wore their human shapes? Signy propped one hand on the railing and stood her ground.

"Hello, Your Grace."

Otto smirked, but said only, "Your Highness. You do understand the purpose of the evening, do you not? You understand why you were brought to Valtyra, why you are allowed to play dress up in the queen's jewels and all this finery."

Signy didn't shout at him, or glare. She looked past him, searching for some sign of rescue. She had chosen her spot for a quiet moment a little too well

Or had Elisa chosen it? Where was Elisa? Where were her guards, for that matter?

"I understand," Signy said stiffly. "I am my grandfather's heir, but in name only. I must marry someone, with his consent, and my husband will be my grandfather's heir."

"The king *and his council* must approve," Otto corrected silkily. "The king *and his council* will choose whether your spouse may inherit the throne. If you throw your choice away on some romantic dream, be assured, it will solve *nothing.*"

Signy gritted her teeth on all the impetuous things she must not say to Otto. She was still trying to figure out what she *should* say when she heard the most welcome sound in the world.

Kai's voice called out through the doorway, "Your Highness?"

Otto take a hasty step back and Signy looked away, out at the sea, so that she wouldn't betray herself completely at the sight of Kai. He was much too handsome in his dress uniform. His blond hair and amber eyes shone brighter than the gold trim when he looked at her.

"Good evening, Your Grace," Kai said politely. "Your Highness, His Majesty is concerned that you are missing your party, and has sent me to escort you back to him."

Signy did dare to look, and she saw certainty in Kai's eyes. *Now.* The time had come.

She allowed herself to smile a little then, knowing that it was almost over. Kai had rescued her now once and for all.

Otto made a little noise, and Signy's gaze darted over to him just in time to see his dawning realization and the hardening scowl. He strode away past Kai, and Signy looked worriedly at Kai as he came to meet her, holding out his hands.

She took them, and felt instantly warm and strong enough to do anything while she had her mate at her side.

"Only one way to go now," Kai murmured to her, squeezing her hands, and then he moved to her side, offering his arm to escort her properly back into the ballroom to be seen by everyone there.

The music was still playing, and there were dancers whirling in beautiful patterns around the floor, but as soon as she stepped into the room Signy's eyes went to the king on his raised dais. The king was watching for her—but Otto was there already at his side, whispering in his ear.

Signy's hand tightened hard on Kai's arm, and Kai murmured, "Courage, Princess."

Signy put her chin up and kept walking, her eyes steady on the king and her spine straight.

Heads turned in her direction as Kai led her on the most direct route to the king. People parted before them, a silence spreading around them. Even the music trailed off when they came to the foot of the royal dais.

The king gestured them closer, and Signy walked up two steps with Kai until they stood directly before the throne. Kai dropped smoothly to one knee, keeping his arm raised for her hand to rest on as Signy stood as straight and tall as she could, meeting the king's eyes directly.

Even Otto had stopped whispering, though he still leaned over the king like some awful shadow. The entire ballroom was silent.

"Well, my dear," the king said. "We have all been waiting for you to choose a suitable partner for your first dance." He raised his eyebrows a little as his gaze dropped to Kai. "The men of the Royal Guard are forbidden from forming attachments, or marrying, without the king's permission to leave his service."

Signy made herself take a long breath in and out to be sure she wasn't interrupting. Then she said, "I know the rules, Your Majesty. But I also know my choice. I have not danced yet because this was not the proper place or time to bring such a weighty matter to you. But if you will give your permission only for tonight, only for a dance, Kai is the partner I would choose. If it please Your Majesty."

There was a short flurry of sound behind her, then silence again. Otto seemed frozen. The king was frowning, his eyes turning down.

Signy's heart raced frantically. If he said no, now, in front of all these people—if he ordered her to dance with someone else—what could she do? What would Kai do?

"Do you let my granddaughter speak for you, guardsman?" The king asked finally.

Kai raised his head to look the king in the eye. "I would not presume to speak before Her Highness, Your Majesty. The choice is hers. But I will lend my voice to her request: if you would release me from my duty for the length of a dance, I would be very glad of the chance to dance with

Princess Signy."

"Hm." The sound the king made was small but definite, his brows drawing down lower.

Otto leaned in, and the king raised one hand in a sharp gesture, warding the First Minister off as sharply as if the king had pushed him back. Otto froze, looking down at that hand, and then straightened up, standing very still.

Signy felt a chill down her spine.

She focused on her grandfather. If he were on her side, her and Kai's side, then they could handle the rest. And what could Otto do here, at a ball, in front of everyone?

"Well," the king said. "It is highly irregular, but I fear that is what one must expect when one permits one's granddaughter to be raised so far away. Very well. You have my permission, both of you—for one dance, and no more. When the music ends, Princess Signy will entertain other partners, and Kai will return to his duties."

Signy felt her face stretch in a grin that no one would have approved as a properly royal expression. Her whole body heated in a flash of dizzy relief and excitement. It wasn't *everything*, but it was a huge step in the right direction—she and Kai wouldn't have to be a secret anymore.

She turned to Kai as he straightened up, tipping her chin back to look up into his face as he grinned back at her. His amber eyes were bright and his gaze was heated.

"Highness," he murmured, turning to guide her back down to the dance floor.

Signy was faintly, distantly aware of people drawing back, watching, but she couldn't look at anyone but her mate, finally here with her in front of everyone so that they could all see what a glorious man she had chosen and been chosen by.

The music started, and Kai drew her into position, his hands guiding her to keep just the right distance and pushing her into the opening steps. He moved strongly, confidently; somewhere in his past with the rough summer jobs there had also been dance lessons.

Signy just stared up at him, smiling helplessly, knowing that someday soon he would be able to tell her all about it—about his family, his *full name*...

He looked back at her with just as much delight, and Signy felt truly at home in her finery as she began to dance in his arms. As strange as she looked to herself in the mirror, she saw a princess reflected in Kai's eyes.

He swept her around the dance floor and she was aware of the rising sounds of people talking, and a few brave couples joining them on the floor. But there would be plenty of time to find out what people thought of her and Kai. For tonight she would only have this one dance to share with her mate.

She couldn't have said how long it went on. It seemed to last forever, and yet she felt like they had only just begun when Kai spun her to a stop and the music ended. Signy stepped back as he released her, dipping into a curtsey as he bowed.

She dropped her gaze to the polished floor, and forced herself to turn half away as soon as she straightened up, because she remembered her promise to the king. One dance with Kai, and then she must dance with other partners.

Stefan was right there, offering her his hand with a wry smile. "I guess now I see why—"

Stefan halted, his eyes going wide, and Signy looked over her shoulder just in time to see a scarlet shape swooping down at her.

She threw her arms up to shield her face, and then there were strong arms around her, hauling her down and sheltering her under a familiar body as the room erupted in screams. She felt something strike Kai as he covered her, and she curled up as small as she could, pressing her face to the front of his uniform.

She could feel a low growl shaking his chest though she couldn't hear it over the sudden chaos. She felt something hit him again, and the growl burst out into a roar as Kai moved above her.

No. He wasn't moving. He was *shifting*.

Huddled on the floor, she stared as his hands became huge golden-furred paws with wicked claws, and looked up to see the enormous lion standing over her. The lion tipped his head back and roared. She saw a red-uniformed form run toward them and recognized Tristan, gesturing urgently to her.

Kai nudged her with one great paw, and she held out her hands to Tristan as he scrambled toward her, letting him pull her clear. A flurry of rustling skirts quickly rallied behind her, and Signy looked up to see Lady Margrethe, her cousin Elisa, and other women she barely recognized gathering into a cordon behind her.

Then her attention was drawn back by a horrible shriek as the scarlet beast on Kai's back spread its wings. Kai reared up under it, roaring again, this time with a depth and power that Signy felt down to her bones. The—it wasn't a bird, but Signy's stunned brain couldn't put a name to it—the scarlet beast was shaken loose but dove at Kai immediately, teeth and talons flashing, tail lashing.

Kai lunged, catching one red leg between his jaws and flinging the creature to the ground, then leaping on it and roaring again. The thing struggled briefly and went limp, and Tristan hissed a curse at Signy's side.

Signy looked over at Tristan, who looked grim and barely disheveled. "We need him alive to speak, but—"

Tristan wasn't the only one who realized Kai was on the verge of killing their attacker. A hulking black wolf leaped into the fight, forcing Kai to let up on the red creature to fling him back with a swipe of his claws—and then Tristan was gone from Signy's side, and a tiger was bounding into the fray.

The fight dissolved into chaos as various animals jumped in. Signy had no idea who any of them were or which side they were on; she only watched for flashes of

Kai's golden fur until she heard the furious roar of a bear, and looked to the royal dais.

A polar bear—her grandfather, looking so like her distant memories of her father that her breath was stolen—stood there, towering at his full height while a brown bear on all fours guarded his flank. A lean gray wolf stood before them, head down as he snarled, and then the king swiped one great paw and Signy turned her face aside, not wanting to see what came next.

Signy! Kai fought his way clear of the melee, and his voice seemed to shake her bones though she knew she wasn't hearing it with her ears. *I don't know who we can trust. We have to get away from here.*

Signy nodded, pushing up to a crouch only to realize as he came to stand before her that the lion's—*Kai's*—back was covered with bleeding gashes. "Kai—"

I'm fine, I'll heal. Climb on, it's the fastest way. We have to get you safe, Kai insisted. *Signy, please.*

Signy nodded and grabbed hold of his thick mane with shaking hands, swinging one leg up over his back. That was enough; Kai made some move that settled her on his back and began to run across the ballroom as the ladies who had guarded Signy's back made way for them.

Signy had a blurred impression of people running for cover or hiding where they could, bird shifters taking flight, and then Kai shot through one of the doorways. He crossed the balcony in a single bound and on the next leap sailed right over the railing.

Signy screamed a little, cutting off abruptly as the lion made an impossibly gentle landing in the garden below. She pressed her face into his mane and held on with her whole body as they raced through the green shadows, the sound of screams and roars fading behind them, and then Kai came to an abrupt halt at a stone wall.

This will only work for one of the royal blood. Do you see the stone that's different?

Signy raised her head and looked, and her eye was

immediately drawn to one of the stones in the wall ahead of them, a little above her eye-level where she was perched on Kai's back. It wasn't a different color than the other stones, wasn't glowing or especially shadowed, but there was an indescribable differentness to it. It was *important*.

Kai didn't have to tell her what to do next. Signy reached out and pressed her hand to that stone. She felt it warm under her touch, an odd flash of recognition, and then she drew her hand back and the stone wasn't there.

The wall wasn't there, either. An open archway looked out over the darkening sky and the dark vast ocean, and on the other side of it a tiny stone platform extended outside the wall.

Signy slid down from Kai's back and stepped through the archway, keeping one hand on her mate as she did. There was enough room to stand, barely, and from here she could see a staircase built into the cliff face, leading down into shadow.

She felt Kai change under her hand and looked back to find that he had shifted to his human form, naked but not badly hurt—at least from the front.

"We shouldn't linger," he said. "I need you to lead the way, Princess. The stones recognize you. They won't let me pass without you, but you can bring me along."

Signy grabbed his hand, then tried to look over his shoulder. "Are you okay? Did they hurt you?"

"I'll be fine," Kai said firmly, squeezing her hand. "There's a boat down below, there will be supplies. We can find somewhere safe to stay until we know who's to be trusted here, but we must not waste time. I don't know who may pursue us."

Signy looked back toward the garden, the lights of the palace. She couldn't hear anything but the ocean now, but she saw two dark shapes burst out through the door they had taken, one leaping over the railing, one taking wing.

"Right," Signy yelped, and turned toward the stairs, still holding tight to Kai's hand.

"Slowly, Princess," Kai told her. "Slow is faster than hurrying out here."

Signy nodded and set her free hand against the stone cliff as she took one step down, then another and another. Kai's hand held hers, and the stone felt warm and reassuring at her side. The roar of the ocean covered anything else she might have heard, and she focused on taking one step after another, down and down and down.

She stumbled when the next step she took wasn't down, but forward. Kai's arm came around her waist, hugging her tightly to him.

"Well done," he said firmly. "Now—"

Something screeched overhead and Kai pushed her down and stood over her, bellowing back a challenge at—whatever it was. Then he tugged her up, hustling her along a stone walkway to where a boat was moored, bobbing gently on the waves. It was a speedboat, just big enough for the two of them, but Signy spotted a promising chest of supplies tucked in the back.

Kai handed her in to the space behind the two seats and reached under a seat, bringing out a black blanket. "Get down, stay under this."

"You—"

"I'm fine, Princess, but I have to get you away from here. *Get down.*"

Signy obeyed, covering up the bright gaudiness of her dress with the dark blanket. She was halfway reassured when Kai wrapped another dark blanket around himself, and then she had the blanket over her head. She muffled another scream into the voluminous fluff of her skirts as the boat leaped into motion, seeming to tip wildly, but she braced herself with her feet against one side and her back at the other. There were a few more wild turns and then they seemed to find their course, speeding forward in what felt like a series of gentle bounces over the surface of the water, like a stone skipping.

After a while even that settled down to a gentler pace,

and she felt Kai tugging at the blanket that covered her. She sat up immediately and then gasped—not at the sight of Kai's face, but at the vast sky above him, streaked with eerie color where it wasn't dappled with brilliant stars.

"Welcome to the north, Your Highness," Kai said, half-shouting above the waves.

Signy knelt up and kissed him as he twisted to face her from his seat, then looked up again, staring as the lights wavered and danced. "It's so beautiful."

She hadn't had a chance to be outside during the short nights so far, and now—though she was aware of the chilly air and the spray of salt water—she never wanted to be anywhere else.

That brought up a question. Signy leaned forward against the back of Kai's seat to speak close to his ear. "Where exactly are we going?"

Kai turned his head, showing her his grin. "I'm taking you home, Princess. You're the Countess of Nordholm, remember? You have your very own castle there. We ought to be able to keep you safe in it until we know what's going on."

10

KAI

Kai's lion rumbled with satisfaction as he led Signy up the short walkway to Nordholm Castle's sea gate. Luckily, it was much closer to sea level than the garden exit from the palace.

Whatever else had happened tonight, everyone had seen him stake his claim to his mate, and now he had brought her safely to a place where he could be sure of protecting her.

"Here, it needs your touch again," Kai said, drawing Signy up to stand tucked against him before the iron-bound gate. "You see where?"

Signy frowned, just as she had at the wall in the palace garden, then nodded and laid her hand on a place that looked like any other to Kai. There was a flash of something like light or heat though it was neither of those, a little burst of magical power into the world. The door swung open, and Signy smiled up at Kai as if he were the one who had made magic for her to delight in.

Kai smiled back and ushered her in, leading her

through the narrow garden of Nordholm Castle, around to the front courtyard where she would be able to get a decent view of the place.

Signy laughed when she saw it, clapping a hand over her mouth as soon as she did.

Kai grinned, showing teeth, and said, "No, you can laugh. It's exactly the place one makes a newborn baby countess of."

Nordholm Castle was too well-built to be a folly—perfectly defensible—but it had never been a fortress. Its footprint was cottage-sized, the first two floors consisting of enough space for four rooms in a plain square. Round towers belled out at each corner with battlements running between them. The towers rose three stories tall on the seaward side, while here on the landward side they stretched a story higher and ended in pointed cupolas with windows all around.

The place was entirely dark: it had been cleaned and stocked in case the princess should wish to visit after her wedding, but there wasn't room for any staff to live in. The local man who bore the title of Castle Warder lived outside the walls with his wife, who did such cooking and housekeeping as might be required by the castle's occupants. She was the one who cooked supper for whatever pair of guardsmen came out to inspect the castle twice a year, as it was a royal holding. They came in through the front gate then, entrusted with a royal warrant and a key.

Signy and the king were the only ones who could come in by the sea gate. Even bird shifters couldn't come in above the walls. The magical wards made Nordholm the safest place in all of Valtyra for Signy right now.

Still, she would be safer, and warmer, indoors. She could hardly be much warmer in her ball gown than Kai was in only a blanket.

Kai looped his arm over her shoulders and drew Signy to the front doors, where she reached out without him having to tell her. Again he felt the little pulse of magic, and then the doors opened before them.

Kai reached over and switched on the lights, revealing the comfortable front room. It was an airy open space decorated in fairly modern style. There were couches and chairs grouped around a fireplace and a pair of chairs angled toward each other convenient to the bookshelves. A deep window seat ran under a pair of high, narrow windows.

Further back was a kitchen—well-stocked, Kai knew—and a dining area that could seat ten comfortably. Nordholm Castle was not built for crowds, but there was plenty of room for family, if...

"Oh," Signy said, looking around wide-eyed. "Oh, it's a *home*, isn't it? And it's mine?"

Kai turned to face her, tugging her as close against him as he could with the skirts of her ballgown in the way. He kissed her lightly and then drew back to see the shining look of happiness in her eyes as she looked up at him. "All yours, Princess-Countess. You could choose to live here, for example, after your wedding."

Signy took a deep breath and sighed it out as she leaned against him, tucking her head against his chest. She set one hand on his arm, the other on his bare side under the blanket wrapped around him—and that seemed to remind her, not just of his nudity, but of all else that had happened tonight.

She pulled back abruptly. "Wait, you were hurt! Are you all right?"

Kai had been managing to ignore it until then, but under Signy's anxious look he winced, aware of the itchy-stinging feeling of healing wounds. "I'll be fine. It's not that bad."

"Let me see!" Signy insisted, then looked around. "Here, or somewhere else?"

"Upstairs," Kai said firmly, smiling as he added, "If you're going to fuss over me, at least let me lie down."

Signy gave him a stern look, and grabbed his hand to tow him toward the stairs. Kai winced again, out of sight behind her, as he climbed.

Now that he wasn't focused on getting Signy to safety, he was more conscious of the pain and the trickle of blood. He tugged the blanket tighter around him, glancing back to be sure he wasn't leaving red footprints.

Signy opened the door to the master suite, which occupied the whole seaward side of the upstairs. Kai looked up from watching his feet to see her look of delight at the long row of windows all looking out to the dark sea and starry sky. Even from here he could see a few ribbons of the Northern Lights still dancing.

Signy marched over to the wide bed and switched on a lamp beside it, washing out the view from the windows and making their reflections appear in the glass instead. She pulled back the covers and Kai hesitated.

They were in Nordholm Castle now, not some American hotel, not sneaking around the palace. This was the princess's own seat, and she was inviting him into her bed here, bloodied and dirty. He kept clutching the blanket around himself as he looked at her in her bedraggled ballgown.

"You should change," he said, trying to cover everything else he wanted to say to her about what this meant.

Signy gave him a mulish look and came back to him, tugging him by the folds of the blanket over to the bed. When she pulled at it, trying to peel it away, Kai gave up and let go. He had known his princess must rule him in some ways, hadn't he? He folded himself onto the bed facedown, and Signy made a little noise of distress.

Her hand touched his shoulder. He turned his head to receive a quick, frowning kiss. "I'll be right back."

He nodded, though in truth he thought he might just fall asleep if she left him here in the quiet. His lion seemed to have already lain down, content to know his mate was here and safe and *his*.

He heard Signy muttering under her breath as she explored the spacious and sybaritic bathroom, then water running, and a moment later she returned to him. He opened his eyes when he felt Signy's weight settle on the mattress at his side, smiling at her.

Signy smiled back, then said, "Tell me if this is too hot?"

She touched a warm cloth to his back. Kai was abruptly entirely awake again. The pain was only a sting, not anything very serious, but every tender touch reawakened it. Signy made a little apologetic sound but her hands kept moving, steady and sure on his back, cleaning what was left of each gouge.

"Do you know what—who—it was?" Signy asked. Her voice shook a little, but her hands kept moving. "Who attacked—"

Kai twisted under Signy's touch and sat up, leaning across the basin of water in her lap to close his arms around her again. "Shh, Princess. You're safe. I'll always keep you safe."

Signy took a sharp breath, nodding against his shoulder. He could almost feel the effort she put into holding back tears. "I know. I just never thought anyone would—not like *that*, not—you're still *bleeding*, Kai, let me—"

Kai tightened his grip, holding Signy until her breathing steadied. He kissed her dark hair—she had lost her tiara when he pulled her to the floor in the ballroom, but her hair was still mostly pulled back in its intricate arrangement. "I'm all right. You're safe, and we're together. That's all that matters right now."

"But who..."

Kai sighed and let go, twisting onto his stomach again.

Signy took the distraction, and he waited until she had made a few passes with the cloth before he said, "I think it was Peter."

Signy froze. "*Peter?* My—the guard? Peter?"

Kai nodded. "He was young, and he had been on the Crown Prince's detail. There weren't many of them, and they didn't mix much with the rest of us. Otto could have gotten to him, convinced him you were a threat to the king. Peter might have thought he was doing the right thing."

Signy sniffed but said nothing, continuing to wash Kai's back. After a moment she said, "But what *was* he? What animal?"

Kai blew out a breath. "Dragon. One of the smaller kinds, thankfully."

Signy went still again, then said in a small voice, "*Dragons are real?*"

Kai turned onto his side so that he could see her face. She was staring down at the bowl of reddened water. Kai took it from her hands and set it on the bedside table, then wrapped his own hands around hers.

"Sorry, I'm being silly," Signy said, her voice shaking again. "You can turn into a lion, my father and grandfather are polar bears, why *shouldn't* dragons be real?"

"You had never seen one before," Kai said gently, keeping his voice low. "And that wasn't a good way to meet one. It's all right to be shocked, Princess. All of this is new to you. We haven't even known each other a week."

Signy shook her head. "It can't have been only a week, I..." Signy straightened up to look him in the eyes. "Kai, whatever else happened tonight, whatever happens next, I can't even pretend there could be anyone else for me. You know that, don't you? I can't do this without you anymore, not another minute."

Kai's lion roared in triumph, but when he leaned in to kiss Signy he touched her tenderly. "I know, Princess. You won't have to. You are mine, and I am yours, no matter what anyone says. If we cannot convince the king, we'll dig in here and let them lay siege, or we'll flee the country, but I won't let you go ever again. I love you."

The words finally wrung something like a sob from Signy, but she kissed him fiercely. "I love you, Kai, I love you so much, but if someone challenges—"

"Don't worry about *that*, Princess," Kai murmured. "I can take care of myself. No one who saw what happened tonight will be eager to start a fight with me when I know it's coming."

Signy shook her head, but she said only, "Can I do anything else for your back? Bandage it?"

Kai didn't want to let her go even as far as the bathroom alone again, but he knew better than to show off and carry her there. He *would* bleed more, and she would fuss just when he might be able to distract her onto a more enjoyable way of spending the night here.

"Come on, I'll find the stuff," Kai said, holding on to Signy as he maneuvered himself back out of the bed. Signy didn't argue this time, and he leaned against her a little as they walked over to the bathroom—mostly, but not entirely, to let her feel like she was helping.

In the bathroom he couldn't ignore the picture they made: himself all bare skin, hard-muscled, and his princess beside him, all pale skin and soft curves, jewels glinting at her throat and wrists, but with obvious smears of blood here and there on her beautiful gown.

She looked like a Valkyrie fresh from the battlefield, every inch worthy of the throne she would someday sit upon.

Kai turned away from that vision to rummage in a cabinet, and soon found the salve he wanted, an ominous-looking dark green with flecks of black. "If you spread this over the wounds, they'll stop bleeding."

"Oh," Signy said, tilting the jar to study it. "Is the black volcanic stone? Valtyra must be a volcanic island, and I suppose if you have it around you could wind up with Quick-Clot as an herbal remedy."

Kai blinked, smiling helplessly. "I'm... not sure what it is, I just know that it works."

"I suppose that's enough to know for now," Signy agreed. She opened the jar, and Kai moved to lean over the counter so that his back would be close to level. He watched her in the mirror, scooping up a generous helping of the salve and laying it into the shallow gouges on his back. He hated the gritty feel of the stuff against raw flesh, but there was no denying that it worked.

And he would suffer much worse to have his mate at his side, tending to him so determinedly. It didn't take long for her to finish; she set the jar down and leaned her elbows on the edge of the sink beside him as she washed her hands. "Now what? Will you be able to lie down?"

"Mm." Kai twisted toward her, kissing at Signy's throat while her hands were occupied. "I could manage, if you wanted me to."

He glanced into the mirror and saw a flush rising on Signy's cheeks, her eyes gone wide and dark and reflecting the lights in a bright ring. "Kai, are you..."

Kai settled his left hand on her back, right over the fastenings of her gown. "We're alone together, Princess. Really alone, with no one to overhear or interrupt. For the first time in how long?"

Signy's eyes drifted shut. "Too long. *Much* too long."

"Then I think we should get you out of this dress," Kai murmured. "And I'll show you what I can do now that you're done fussing over me."

Signy reached back with both hands, staying bent under Kai's hand, and undid the top button at the back of her dress. Kai followed her lead, unbuttoning the next several before they gave way to a hidden zipper. Signy lowered her hands, letting Kai take over as he eased the zipper down to reveal bare skin and then the stern-looking thing she was wearing underneath, halfway between a bra and a corset.

It was going to require both hands to unfasten, so Kai moved over, pressing his hips against the skirts that still kept him from Signy's backside. She pushed back against him, making Kai's whole body feel hotter, his lion growling with need for his mate, but Kai focused on undoing the whole long row of little hooks, revealing Signy's skin, inch by inch, alternately pale and pink where the garment had pressed hard against her.

He stroked his fingers over the indented marks, drawing a sweet, low noise from Signy's throat, and then he was at the waist of her dress and had to figure out what fastened where.

"It goes up from there," Signy told him after a moment. "Up over my head."

Kai grunted, not wanting to move away from her for a moment, and then he started to pull the skirts up. Signy laughed a little but cooperated, reaching down to pull them forward where she still leaned over the sink. For a moment his mate disappeared under a froth of upended dress, but then between them they managed to get Signy free of it and shove the dress to the floor.

That left Signy still bent over the sink wearing only her necklace and bracelets above the waist and panties below, with thigh-high stockings attached to them by ribbons with clips at either end. Kai leaned into her, pressing his cock against the soft rounds of her backside under her panties, resting his chest against her bared back.

Signy bowed her back under him, tipping her head back to look back at him. She reached back to sink one hand into his hair, and that made room for Kai to slide his hands under her, cupping his hands under the delicious weight of her breasts.

Signy moaned softly at his touch, tilting her head. Kai nuzzled at her throat, pale under the richness of gold and rubies still wrapped around it. He kissed her delicate skin and rubbed at her stiff nipples with his thumbs, rocking his hips against her.

"Yes," she breathed. "Kai, oh, please, I'm yours, show me I'm yours."

"All mine," he promised her, biting just a little harder and then licking over the spot. He kept his hands moving on her breasts, then finally made himself let go, sliding his hands down the soft curve of her belly and sides to the top of her panties. "And still a little overdressed, Princess."

"All this protocol to learn..." Signy's words trailed off into a pleased sound as Kai peeled her panties down, backing up just enough to make room as he did. He got down on his knees to draw her stockings down, and then he couldn't resist the hot, wet smell of her, so ready for him.

He slid two fingers inside her, just to feel how wet she was, how readily she received him. Signy gasped at the touch. He could feel her whole body respond, more wetness blooming over his knuckles from just that first touch. He had to have more.

He stood again, and guided Signy to turn to face him. She gave a sweet little frown, and then he boosted her up to sit on the edge of the counter.

She covered her mouth with her hand as Kai sank back down to his knees, pressing her thighs apart to open her for him, and Signy leaned back against the mirror, making little muffled sounds while he was still nuzzling at the dampness that slicked her inner thighs.

When he moved further in, nosing at her damp curls and licking the pink folds of her, Signy moaned out loud, gasping his name at his first long lick. Kai rumbled back a pleased noise with the taste of his mate's desire on his tongue.

He went on licking and teasing her until Signy slid one hand into his hair and tugged hard, making him look up to meet her dark eyes, wide and dazed. "Kai, please, don't make me wait."

Kai groaned and moved, standing up to lean in and kiss her hard. Signy clung to him with her whole body, her hands on his arms while her thighs tightened around his hips, trying to draw him in the rest of the way. Kai shifted his hips to line himself up and drew back from kissing just to hear the sweet needy sound Signy made as he entered her.

Signy's hand came up to the back of his neck, clinging to him as he slid into the wet heat of her, inch by inch. He fit so snugly inside her, and he had never felt more right than like this, joined with his mate. He brushed teasing kisses over her lips as he filled her up. Signy sighed against him, surrendering to him until he was fully inside her.

Kai braced one hand against the mirror and started to move inside her, putting his other arm around her to cradle her close. Signy moaned and held on tighter, squeezing his cock inside her and wringing an answering groan from Kai.

"Mine," he breathed in her ear, thrusting harder inside her. "My mate, my princess, always."

"Always," Signy promised. "Kai, always, always—"

She ground up against him, finding her own pleasure. Kai growled and kissed her harder, shifting the angle of his hips until he could feel every thrust echoing through her body. He lifted his head when he felt her getting close, watching the ecstasy reflected on her face as it got better and better, building higher with every movement of their bodies together.

"Come on, darling," he whispered. "It's all right, I've got you—"

Signy gasped, then gave a little cry and arched under him. He felt the pulse of her as she climaxed, her body tightening fiercely on his. It swept his own mounting pleasure right over the edge, and he pressed deep inside her as he came, his seed pulsing out inside his mate.

"Mine," he whispered again as he came down, kissing gently at her flushed cheeks, her parted lips. "Mine, Signy, all mine."

"My mate," Signy smiled up at him, then frowned a little and ran one hand gingerly over his back. Kai looked over his shoulder, but saw the same as he felt: the gouges had stopped bleeding, and would finish healing soon.

"Come on," he murmured, slipping free of her body

and kissing her one more time. "Let's get to bed, Princess."

Signy nodded, her eyelids already looking heavy. She let Kai guide her to the bed and lay her down.

He curled himself around her, his lion's instinct to protect all the more determined now. She was his, really his, and wouldn't choose any other. He didn't know yet what that would mean, but that was a problem for tomorrow. Tonight he would sleep soundly with his mate in his arms.

11

SIGNY

Signy woke up with Kai's hot naked body wrapped around hers, and a delicious soreness between her legs. For a moment she felt nothing but the gladness of being with her mate—her own, her one and only. Light flooded the room, and she blinked at the unfamiliar surroundings, snuggling close to Kai as her eye caught on the dazzling expanse of the ocean visible outside the windows.

Home, she thought. *I'm home, and you're here, and I don't need anything else.*

Kai nuzzled sleepily at her throat and behind her ear, and Signy laid her arms over his and smiled, wanting nothing more.

Then she heard a booming sound, like the knock of a very large fist on a very large door. She jerked fully awake as Kai stiffened and tightened his grip.

All at once she remembered the night before: dancing with Kai until they were attacked—by *Peter* in his *dragon shape*—and the ballroom dissolving into chaos as shifters fought each other. Her grandfather in his bear form, roaring as Kai carried her away, straight to a boat that sped across the waves in the night to this refuge.

And now, clearly, someone had come looking for them. "Kai? What do we do?"

Kai blew out a breath and sat up, keeping one hand on her shoulder as he looked around. The sound didn't repeat, and she didn't hear anything else but the crashing of the waves. Kai stood up and walked decisively over to a door that proved to be a closet. He took out a quilted robe of red silk and held it up for her. "Here, Princess, put something on."

The only clothes Signy had actually brought with her were the ballgown and underwear abandoned on the bathroom floor, so she was lucky there was anything stocked here. She stood and went to Kai, letting him help her into the robe. He touched her hair, which seemed to still be mostly in place from the night before, and Signy looked up at him, remembering his help in getting her ready to face her first appearance in Valtyra.

"I'll be right beside you," he murmured. Signy turned to face him, looking up and down his naked body.

"*You* need clothes," she pointed out, glancing into the closet again.

Kai nodded and gestured toward the door. "There are a few spare uniforms in one of the other rooms."

Signy gave him a little push, following on his heels when he moved in that direction. She stayed in the doorway as he retrieved a pair of dark pants and a shirt and jacket from another closet. Kai glanced warily at the front windows—that must have been the direction that the knocking sound came from—but he said nothing about who he thought it might be, only dressed quickly.

Once he was dressed—without shoes, so Signy didn't feel so bad about not having any either—he offered her his arm and escorted her down the stairs. She remembered the way he had escorted her, just the night before, across the king's ballroom. Her hand tightened on his arm and she said, "Kai, *who is it?*"

The knocking sounded again. Now Signy could tell that they were pounding, not on the door of the little castle itself, but on the gate in the wall that surrounded it.

Kai shook his head slightly. "I don't know. Much depends on how many guards Otto had convinced to join him. If the king was badly hurt, or if someone took the chance to declare a proper challenge..."

Signy felt cold inside, thinking of what might have happened while she was here, making love with Kai.

They reached the front door. Kai moved ahead of her to open it while blocking her from the opening.

"Kai!" someone shouted immediately. "Your Highness! We brought clothes, and breakfast!"

"*Laila?*" Signy said, startled, and she saw relief dawn on Kai's face and knew he must have been worried for his sister's safety.

"Who's we?" Kai called back, his voice sounding stern. He still kept himself between Signy and the open door.

"Someone you can trust," Tristan called out, and now Kai's shoulders sagged with real relief. He smiled at Signy and led her out into the little courtyard, crossing to the gate to let them in.

Signy gasped at her first sight of Tristan. He was in a neater version of the same uniform Kai wore—with boots on, even—but two ugly cuts marred the side of his face, and there was a bandage on the side of his throat, as well.

His eyes darted quickly to her and he bowed, touching his hand to his heart. "Your assailant has been captured and has confessed all he knows. You are safe again in Valtyra, I swear it."

Tristan had been in the thick of the fight in his tiger form. He must have taken the brunt of it once Kai turned away to help her escape.

"Thank you," Signy said, forgetting every bit of protocol she'd been drilled on. She reached out to touch Tristan's arm instead, pressing an impulsive kiss to his uninjured cheek. She quickly stepped back to Kai's side, and added, "Please, come in, both of you."

Tristan stepped back to usher Laila in. She was towing a distractingly modern bright purple roller suitcase, and she looked between them and said, "Oh, thank goodness. *Kai!*"

Kai glanced over at Signy as he stepped forward to hug Laila, and Signy folded her arms and raised her eyebrows, fighting a smile as she waited for his explanation. But Kai said only, "Signy—my sister, Laila, I think you know each other? Laila—my mate, Signy."

Laila huffed and smacked Kai's arm. "You could have *told* me, you know! I wouldn't have given you two away. Not that you didn't do an impressive job of it yourselves last night."

Tristan stepped through the gate with a paper grocery bag in each hand, and Laila darted around behind him to pull the gate shut. "Breakfast," Tristan said, nodding toward the castle doors. "And then we'll tell you what's awaiting back in the city."

Kai's expression turned serious, and Signy felt her own shoulders straighten instinctively. She and Kai couldn't actually hide here for long. The rest of the world was bound to intrude.

But Tristan was right. They might as well eat first.

Tristan, like Kai, seemed familiar with what could be found where in Castle Nordholm. They were soon sitting down to a complete meal from covered dishes in the paper bags. Signy took a few bites, then broke the silence by saying, "It seems the palace kitchens, at least, continue on as normal?"

Laila smiled crookedly. "By and large, yes, though the cooks are as worried as everyone else."

Kai took Signy's hand under the table and squeezed it firmly. "Tell us, then."

Tristan shook his head and swallowed his bite of bread. "It's not irretrievable, I don't think. The king bloodied Otto and placed him under arrest, but he escaped. We didn't get to all of the servants he'd suborned quickly enough, and they managed to take Nikolai as well. One of the servants we did catch confessed to helping Otto tamper with the king's medicines, so we know that was deliberate, though that hardly matters next to last night. Otto and Nikolai have both been declared outlaws already. I don't envy Magnus dealing with INTERPOL, but they won't dare show their noses *here* again."

"Nikolai?" Signy asked tentatively.

"Another nephew of Otto's—a big black wolf," Kai filled in. "In the Guard, but obviously he was not as clear as he should have been about being loyal to the crown before his family."

Tristan made an odd equivocating noise. "I was there for part of Peter's confession. Magnus and the king went in to question him personally, and with those two in front of him he broke and started crying and apologizing and spilling everything within five minutes. He insists that Otto showed him proof that Signy was a pretender, not even the prince's daughter, and she was poisoning the king with human medicines and controlling his mind, and you were in on it as well. So he thought he was being loyal, even if what he was was a young idiot."

Kai shook his head grimly, but Signy felt oddly relieved. She would rather believe the young guard had been misled than that he had schemed against her as coldly as Otto had, even if the end result was the same.

"He named a few others who will be watched carefully, but all have renewed their oaths of allegiance." Tristan smiled with the uninjured side of his mouth and added, "And we've already had a volunteer to fill one of the vacancies in the guard—Stefan Sparre af Varg fought by my side last night, and swears he knew nothing of his uncle's true plans, which Peter hasn't contradicted. Stefan has offered to renounce his name and join the guard to make up for his uncle and his cousin Nikolai. He asked me to tell you so directly, Your Highness."

"Oh," Signy touched her fingers to her mouth, thinking

of Stefan in a different light. He had been kind, and polite, and if he truly hadn't known—had helped Tristan against Peter and Nikolai—then he deserved the chance to prove himself.

She looked over at Kai, wondering if he would dislike having someone who had courted her take a place among the Royal Guard, but he just squeezed her hand again. "It might be good for him, at that. Royal service has a way of bringing a man to where he ought to be."

Signy nodded cautiously, then looked back to Tristan. That couldn't be all the news he had.

"Magnus?" Kai asked.

Tristan nodded. "He has stayed at the king's side continually. The king's only public word has been that he will speak to no one else until Princess Signy returns home. I haven't seen him since he left Peter's confession. The council are scattered, fled abroad or hunkering down on their country estates, and the rumors are flying—one of which is that Otto chose *you* to take to America and set you to seduce the princess."

Signy froze, and for a second she couldn't read Kai's face at all.

Then Kai shook his head, drawing Signy closer to his side. "Well, if he were able to invent mating bonds where none would have been, I suppose I would have to thank him for bringing me to Signy. But if he expects a pardon in exchange, he'll be waiting a long time."

Tristan snorted and nodded. "I saw the two of you when you'd newly recognized each other. *I* know the truth, and Laila obviously knows enough to trust you, but no one really knows the princess and not many know *you* very well, Kai."

"The king knows me. And Magnus knows me." Kai was still holding on tight to Signy, as if someone might try to take her from him by force right now. Signy laid her hand over his.

She wasn't letting him go again either. Never again.

Tristan nodded as well. "But neither of them is speaking to anyone now, so you see how it is."

Kai sighed and nodded, then looked down at Signy. "Well, Princess? Shall we go and face the music?"

Signy realized that it was a genuine question. If she told him she wanted to go back to America now, or stay hidden here, he would stay with her, or go. The thought of returning to the capitol and trying to make everyone accept her and Kai, to believe that their bond was true, when she knew that it all really could turn to outright fighting again...

And yet, she had come this far, and she couldn't just give up with the job half done.

"As long as we're facing it together," Signy said, and Kai smiled and kissed her lightly.

"Always, Princess," he murmured.

"Well, then, you're both going to need to change your clothes," Laila said practically, and Signy blushed at the reminder that they had an audience.

But Tristan and Laila were both watching them with amusement, and they had both come so far to help. Kai wasn't the only one she could depend on through whatever came next.

~~*

The drive back to the capitol took less time than getting dressed and having her hair fixed to Laila's satisfaction. It was still only mid-morning when the palace on its clifftop came into view, and Tristan said, "I think this would be a good place for you to get out and walk, Your Highness."

They had discussed the strategy of this while Signy was getting dressed: the most important thing right now was for people to see that Signy was safe, and alive, and that she was with Kai of her own free will. Keeping secrets was no longer an advantage. Now Signy needed to be seen and known by as many of her people as possible.

Signy nodded to Tristan, and Kai, sitting beside her, squeezed her hand. She looked over at him—resplendent again in a clean copy of his shiny dress uniform from the night before. Signy was wearing a gold-embroidered white dress, much simpler than her ball gown, falling just to her knees. She had put her bracelets from the night before back on, but left the heavy formal necklace off. Laila hadn't brought any jewelry out of the palace for her, but her hair combs had sparkling red and gold decorations that would catch the morning light.

"Okay," Signy said, taking a breath. "Let's do this."

"We'll be right behind you," Tristan assured her, and Signy nodded.

Kai reached over and opened the car door and got out, offering his hand to help her as she followed.

There weren't many people around, but when Signy stepped out of the car she found that they were already all staring at her. She smiled and waved at them, as if this were a perfectly normal occasion, then looked around the street. It was a broad avenue, tree-lined, that led through a downtown shopping area here and up to the gates of the palace.

"Let's go," she said firmly. Kai nodded crisply, angling his arm for her to rest her hand on it.

Signy put her chin up and started walking down the middle of the street, leading a parade that consisted, so far, only of Tristan following in the black car about ten feet behind them.

She looked around as she walked. She hadn't been out into the city at all in the last few days; she had been so busy with cram sessions and dress fittings and being introduced to unwanted suitors that she hadn't met many ordinary Valtyrans, and none of them had seen her since the day she stepped off the plane.

A few voices called out, "Princess Signy! Princess Signy!"

Signy looked around and smiled, waving when she met

anyone's eyes. Some looked delighted, some dumbfounded. Everyone had their phones out, and doors kept opening, bringing more people to the sidewalks. Traffic on the other side of the street stopped as people pulled over to watch her walking.

She glanced over at Kai, walking steady and calm at her side. No one called out his name, and she wondered if people knew it, if he was someone any of them would recognize.

She wondered what his name *was*. Technically he was still a guardsman, so although he'd named his connection to Laila, he still hadn't told Signy his full name or anything about the rest of his family.

Soon. They were less than a mile from the palace now. The road ahead of them was perfectly clear of traffic, while the sidewalks were filling up fast. The voices calling out quickly became too numerous for Signy to make out exactly what anyone was saying, but she kept waving, kept smiling.

Kai's hand tightened as they reached a cross street. She almost didn't notice, because people were standing all the way across that street, blocking any possible traffic. But when she looked, Signy recognized a sleek black car waiting at the corner.

Signy stopped, looking up at Kai. She couldn't read his expression, and she knew better than to look back toward Tristan, who she knew would be poised to jump in at the first sign of a threat.

In the next moment the doors of the black car opened, and three more men in red uniforms got out, plus one in a black suit. Two were guards whose names Signy couldn't remember, and the third was Andrej, who had often guarded the doors of her room. The man in the suit was Stefan, and she saw that one hand and wrist were heavily bandaged.

"Steady," Kai murmured under his breath. "Steady, Princess."

All four men came away from the car and dropped to one knee, and Signy heard a silence spread out. Everyone who saw what was happening in the street went silent.

Signy stared for a moment, and then made the small gesture releasing them from their bow.

All four stood and got into motion—Andrej and another guard took up positions several feet in front of her and Kai, to either side, clearing their path. The third guard and Stefan fell back, to walk just behind the car Tristan was still driving behind them.

"Well," Signy said, stepping forward again with Kai at her side. "*Now* it's a parade."

Kai cracked a smile as he looked down at her, and Signy was startled when the silence around them was broken by a cheer. Kai actually looked around for the first time then, and Signy slid her hand down his arm to hold his hand, raising it up for people to see.

The cheering got louder.

Signy couldn't hold back a little laugh, and after that she and Kai walked hand in hand. A few times Kai raised his free hand to wave a little, and Signy thought she detected louder cheers just for him. At the very least, no one seemed *unhappy* to see him at her side.

The palace was starting to loom large in her sight when Andrej and the other guard walking ahead looked at each other and then back at Signy—at Kai, Signy quickly realized, because he made a little gesture back at them, and Andrej turned and jogged past them to move behind them. Signy let herself look back then, following his motion, and realized why.

The people they passed were falling in behind them, filling the street and marching after Signy to the palace.

"*Now* it's a parade," Kai murmured, squeezing her hand. A couple of blocks after that four more red-uniformed guards stepped out of the crowd. These walked all the way out into the street to stand facing Signy, and once again Signy and Kai—and the whole parade behind them—stopped to see what they would do, and a silence fell.

The crowd roared when the guards knelt, and Signy quickly gestured for them to rise. They spread out in crisp movements, making a rank of three walking ahead of Signy, one falling back to help behind, and two others walking well to either side of Signy and Kai.

Their parade moved on smoothly for another half-block, and then Signy heard Kai's breath catch. She looked to see what he'd seen, and found that he was staring at a tall man with golden blond hair standing with a short, plump woman whose hair was pale flax, like Laila's.

"Are they..."

"They are," Kai said, hesitating a second. He raised his hand to wave as he finished, "Laila's parents."

Which meant they were *Kai's* father and stepmother. Signy waved too, and saw both of them smile and wave frantically back. Signy looked at Kai's face, the uncertain hope shining in his eyes, and she thought that she and Laila would have to work together to bring Kai back to his family. But at least they were here, cheering him on, even when they couldn't claim him.

Kai looked down at her and squeezed her hand in his, and then looked up again with a steadier smile, walking on and waving to everyone.

It seemed as if the entire city must have converged by the time they were walking the last few blocks up to the palace gates, which stood open, with more red-uniformed guards waiting to either side.

They were still half a block from the gates when a man in a black suit walked out from one side, accompanied by just one man in a red uniform. The whole crowd fell silent, and then all the people sank down at once, men going to one knee while women dipped into low curtseys.

The king, who had so rarely been seen by the public even within the palace in recent years, now stood before them, looking tall and strong and thoroughly in command.

149

He wore the same simple gold circlet he had worn to the ball.

Signy glanced over at Kai, who was standing very steady and still holding firmly to her hand. When he tugged, she stepped forward with him, exactly in sync. They would do this together or not at all; there was no other choice either of them would consider, now.

When she was close enough to see the sharpness in her grandfather's brown eyes as well as the sternness of his expression, Signy stopped again and dipped into her own low curtsey. At her side, Kai dropped to one knee, but still held on to her hand.

Signy watched the king's feet and his hands. She saw when he took a step forward and then another, rather than signaling her and Kai to rise. She concentrated on holding her curtsey, acutely aware of the silent audience behind them.

The king stopped just in front of her, and still didn't signal her to rise from her curtsey. Instead he reached out and touched her chin, drawing her face up to meet his eyes.

He smiled, and Signy knew. It was all she could do not to laugh out loud with joy. *Yes, yes! Yes!*

She straightened up when the king beckoned, but Kai stayed on one knee.

The king turned toward him, while Signy stood at his side still holding on to his hand.

"Guardsman," the king said, in a carrying voice that would reach the crowd. "You have returned my granddaughter, the Princess Royal of Valtyra, safely to me, after protecting her from assassins in my own palace last night. Anything you ask of me now, I will give."

"Your Majesty," Kai replied, and even with his head bowed he made his voice boom so that Signy felt it in her bones, and she knew the crowd would hear as well. "I ask only to be released from your service, so that I may marry my true mate and continue to serve Valtyra at her side."

The king smiled and glanced past them at the crowd before he said, still in a voice for the crowd, "I hope, after all this running about, that you mean Princess Signy."

A little laughter rippled through the crowd, breaking the silence. Kai glanced up at Signy, his amber eyes bright as gold and a smile curving his mouth. He turned his head down again properly as he said, "I do, Your Majesty."

"Then arise," the king said. "No more to deny your name and family in my service, but to increase it. Lord Konstantin Rikard Natt och Dag af Leijona, you have my blessing to marry my granddaughter, Princess Signy of Valtyra."

Kai stood, unfolding to his full height, as the crowd roared their approval. He touched his hand to his heart, mouthing a last, private *thank you*, to the king, and then turned to Signy and met her eyes.

She had thought she had seen the fullness of his power when she saw him in lion form, but Kai standing before her, free to claim his name and his mate, was a new man all over again. She felt a fresh thrill of heat, her knees going a little weak, and she clung to him as he leaned in and kissed her.

Signy didn't know whether the crowd roared louder then, or if the noise she heard was the thunder of her own pounding heart. It didn't matter. She was in Kai's arms, and she never had to give him up again.

12

SIGNY

The ceremony to make Kai—*Lord Konstantin Rikard Natt och Dag af Leijona*—officially the Crown Prince, and Signy officially his Crown Princess, took place two days later. By then, not only were Kai's father and stepmother sitting in the front row with Laila, but Signy's mother and stepfather were sitting with them.

Signy had found a string of increasingly worried text messages from her mother when she finally thought to look at her phone again after returning from Nordholm. One of them had said, *Honey, he didn't say anything about your bio dad, did he?*

Signy had called her mother to explain everything, only to hear her mother's newly-recorded voicemail message. "If this is Signy, honey, I'm on my way to Copenhagen and I'll be there as soon as I can. If it's anybody else—sorry, I'm going to be in Europe for a while."

Signy's parents had arrived that night. Signy's didn't think anything could surprise her more than the fact that they came at all, until she saw her stepfather appearing to take it all in stride, other than looking uncomfortable in what was obviously a new suit. Signy had never seen him wear anything more formal than clean sandals and jeans without holes before.

Then her mother turned to the king and started giving him a piece of her mind about whisking Signy away without consulting her. Signy decided right then to just stop being surprised by anything at all.

It had taken a while to explain everything. Signy had felt close to tears at the sudden display of protectiveness from her mother, belated as it was. She had come, without Signy even having to ask.

She had even agreed to wear a tiara to Kai and Signy's investiture as Crown Prince and Crown Princess. Signy was wearing one, too, though not the delicate one she had worn to her first ball, which had been rather badly damaged in the melee and was still being studied by the royal jewelers to decide how best to restore it.

This time Signy wore a heavier circlet of diamonds and pearls, along with embroidered ceremonial robes that made her ballgown feel like a nightgown in comparison. But Kai was at her side, wearing a heavily embroidered cloak and receiving a gold circlet on his tawny hair, and Signy felt light enough to fly when he took her hand and kissed it, vowing to rule Valtyra by her side.

~~*

Afterward there was a luncheon on a scale that almost did seem private to Signy by then—barely twenty people, just the king and his council, the councilors' spouses, and her and Kai's family and closest friends. Plus the ever-present guardsmen, of course.

"I wish Poppy were here," Signy said, surveying the gathering of people in the room. She looked up at Kai from under the weight of her crown and added, "I wish I could make her a princess, too. We made you a prince, you'd think that could be arranged."

Kai glanced over at his own sister, who was deep in conversation with their father. Now that Kai would inherit the throne of Valtyra, Laila—*Lady* Laila Natt och Dag af Leijona—was her father's only heir. Poppy, on the other hand, was traveling the world by taking intermittent jobs under the table whenever she ran out of money.

"Oh, this again," Signy's mom said, shaking her head. "You were hung up on that for weeks after she was born, wanting her to be a princess since you and I already were. That was part of the reason I stopped talking about it, and discouraged you from talking about it—I never wanted Poppy to feel less special than the magic princess in the family."

Signy shook her head. Redheaded, fearless Poppy had always seemed so much more special than Signy. It was hard to believe her mother had worried about the opposite.

"Still," her mother added, "she just posted one of those messages about *Don't worry if you don't hear from me for a few weeks!* So I can't argue with wishing she was here."

Signy realized guiltily that she hadn't had time to check on her sister's Instagram in days. And now there was probably no way to get in touch with her at all. Her wedding to Kai was the day after tomorrow, and there was no way anyone could track her down before then.

"Well," Kai said slowly, and Signy looked up at him.

Kai glanced over at Tristan this time. His wounds had healed, leaving only fading scars on his cheek and throat.

"One of your guards does have *some* experience with going in search of young American ladies and persuading them to come to Valtyra," Kai offered. "And even if Poppy isn't in the line of succession, she *is* your sister. That makes her a part of the royal family, I would think. Maybe she ought to have the Royal Guard's protection? Especially..."

Kai trailed off and met Signy's eyes with a serious expression. She had managed not to tell her mother just how dangerous things had gotten for her, or that Otto and Nikolai were still out there somewhere. But Otto might well know who Poppy was after tracking Signy down in America, and with that thought Signy was utterly determined to bring her sister home, at least for the time being.

She looked toward Tristan, who seemed to sense they were talking about him. His gaze settled on Signy and he frowned slightly.

Signy made herself smile back, and the smile turned sincere as she thought of the serious guard chasing after her wild baby sister to deliver an invitation from Signy. Even though Signy only had eyes for her mate, she was pretty sure that Tristan would have no trouble getting Poppy's attention. Poppy wouldn't put up with being *brought* back to Valtyra for her own safety, but she could probably be lured, and Tristan would do the job... handsomely.

She turned to her grandfather, seated on her opposite side, waiting until he finished murmuring something to Magnus and noticed her. He smiled at her, and Signy smiled back and said, "Grandfather, could I ask a favor?"

THE END

ABOUT THE AUTHOR

Zoe Chant loves writing paranormal romance! Over a hot cup of tea (or something stronger), she whips up sexy tales of hunky heroes and adventurous heroines to tantalize and satisfy her readers. Sizzling hot romance, no cliffhangers!

Join Zoe's mailing list to receive email notifications about her new releases:
http://eepurl.com/bhOy_T

Printed in Great Britain
by Amazon